ILLUSIONS

By

Jacqui Jacoby

BODY COUNT
PRODUCTIONS, INC.

© 2016 by Jacqui Jacoby, Body Count Productions, Inc.

All rights reserved. No part of this book may be reproduced, stored in a retrieval system, or transmitted in any form, or by any means, electronic, mechanical, photocopying, recording or otherwise, without prior permission of the author.

This is a work of fiction. Names, characters, places and incidents either are products of the author's imagination or are used fictitiously. Any resemblance to actual events or locales or persons, living or dead, is entirely coincidental. I rest my case.

The author acknowledges the use of various trademark words in this work including and not limited to IHOP, Denny's, Snapple, Oreo, Victoria Secrets, Future Frank, Pontiac and more.

Library of Congress: 2015916509

ISBN print: 978-0-9966157-9-2

ISBN e-book: 978-0-9967678-0-4

First Edition 2016.

www.bodycountproductionsinc.com

DEDICATION

Joanne Firby

~ because she didn't ask why I needed a hovercraft full of eels ~

ACKNOWLEDGEMENTS

Larry Wilson

Scene Idea Consultant

Bridgette Wilson

for the rescue

Editing by Nas Dean

nas_dean@ymail.com

Cover Design

by

Angie Waters

based on a design by Bridgette Wilson

ADDITIONAL STORY OFFERINGS

Judd Spittler

Susan Andersen Stone

Sabrina K. Buie

CHAPTER ONE

Sitting in the jump seat of a van with mesh covered windows, Trevor Martin let them buckle him in, thinking how much he truly hated the orange color.

If he had a chance, it would be the last color he ever put on his body again.

"Why the transfer?" He asked the guard across from him. The driver stared at the road; the guard in front didn't turn around.

"Because of shut the fuck up."

"Clever," Trevor smiled. "Can I know where I have to go at two o'clock in the morning? No one told me about this."

"Is there a part of what I said you didn't understand?"

Trevor closed his eyes and let his head fall back.

Over five years ago everything that was normal died. Trevor became a man he didn't know he was. He did things he didn't know he could and he never regretted them. Not even when he was caught, arrested, and tossed in a little cell by himself.

Tried with his cousin—Gavin—they were kept apart since the verdict was read. Not only they lost everyone else, they lost each other when each other was all they had. Raised as brothers who had shared everything from toys, to jeans, to date stories, now they were sharing one more thing.

They were serving a life sentence with no possibility for parole.

They were never going to see each other again.

The van pulled into a darkened lot near a wired and barbed fence. Trevor, with his back to the door, didn't know it was Gavin loaded in, until Gavin had been secured across from him. He looked as shocked as Trevor felt.

It had been over a year since they had sat at that table with their lawyers. Gavin looked good. Thinner, but good. Even in orange.

They stared at each other.

"Any clue?"

Trevor thinned his lips tight and shook his head.

"Great," Gavin sighed hard, looking to the side. "So not good."

They drove for two hours in a silence as total as any Trevor could remember.

The terrain changed from city to rural until the van started up into the hills. Probably easier to throw the body in a ditch in the middle of nowhere.

New Jersey didn't have the death penalty...at least not before now.

Mom. Aunt Lucy. Emily. Jayce. Caleb. Sarah. Baby Lucas.

The names that he never dared remember slipped into his mind.

All of them sharing a gravesite at Baywater Cemetery. Mom had been forty-two. Lucas was fifteen months, everyone else in between.

Trevor looked at Gavin.

"Remember the last Christmas?"

Gavin smiled and nodded his head. "Mom tried that turkey she got on discount."

"Piece of leather with wings," Trevor laughed. "God, it was awful."

"Hey, shut the fuck up back there."

"Why?" Trevor snapped, turning to look at the guard. "Harder to shoot us in here than out there?"

The guard had his hand on his gun, but backed down.

"You never told her," Gavin said.

"She tried so hard and was so proud. I couldn't take that from her and you should talk. You had seconds."

They both, shackled to the floor, laughed hard.

"Regrets?" Trevor asked.

Gavin looked to the back of the van and then at Trevor, his chin tilted and he grinned.

"I still think we should have gone to IHOP."

They were arrested in a Denny's. Trevor smiled as the van pulled off and took a dirt road.

It stopped in a clearing and the lights went off.

One car waited, its headlights on.

A woman got out carrying a silver briefcase and headed toward them. It was near black, but he wasn't so confused he couldn't tell she was gorgeous enough to make every man here think twice.

Armed guards and two convicted murderers standing in front of the van.

And yet she walked right up.

"Are you armed?" the guard asked.

"Of course I'm not armed, you moron," she snapped.

He took a step toward her. "I'm going to have to search you."

"Oh, in your dreams," she laughed. "Take five steps back now or I walk with the case."

"And the three of you could be shot trying to escape and I still get the case."

"Yeah, that's true," she smiled. "But I still have the rest in the account you are hoping to get your grubby little hands on. Why settle for the case when I can provide more?"

"How much more?"

She raised her arms and sent the case airborne into the guard's chest.

"Not a dime. Gimme the keys," she said in a voice that made her looks pale.

"They're murderers. You don't want to do this."

"Since I've already come this far, it would appear I do want to do this so hand me the keys."

"They will kill you."

"That's my business."

Gavin leaned close toward Trevor. "What's happening?"

Trevor stayed focused and tried not to think too positively.

"And maybe it's my business to take this bribe, arrest you and take you back with all of us."

"Sure. That's your choice. I am sure Mark is going to appreciate it."

"Who the fuck is Mark?"

"Your eight year old nephew who will grow up in foster care when his mom and dad are busted for drug trafficking with the evidence already planted on their computer. I might toss in some prostitution on that one. Your sister looks like a slut."

Trevor's chuckles mixed in with Gavin's. The guard smacked Trevor on the back of the head.

"What?" the other guard snapped at her.

She pointed to the goon next to him. "Nancy will lose that scholarship she just earned when the photos come out and trust me, I didn't manufacture the photos. I just found them on the Internet. Three guys at once? I am sure the college will love it and offer her a position somewhere on campus doing something special."

Guns came up, aimed and cocked, all in her direction.

"Or you could do that," she said in that sweet voice, "and his nephew, Seth, will not only be expelled from USC for paganism, but he will also do time for drug trafficking. I put him on a timer and it's running."

"You fucking bitch."

She took a step forward, closing the distance. "Yes, that's right. I am a fucking bitch with more computer capabilities than your pathetic mind can handle. So I will take what I paid for, and I will leave you all alone. But if I see a hint of shadow behind any of us ever, I will take apart everyone you love and leave you alone so you can watch and know who is behind it. And it will be your fault because you were worried about me and my two new friends."

"Ohh," Trevor muttered. He looked at Gavin. "Our side?"

"God, I hope so."

"Why?" the guard snapped. "They're fucking murderers."

"What would you do if some jerks went to your house on a mistake and killed your wife and five kids—Alice, Jamie, Stewart, Paul and Rachel, by the way—what would you do if they aimed wrong and took them all away? Bring flowers to their graves?"

"That shit doesn't happen. Not to me," he snapped.

"Shut up," the other guard choked, looking at her. "You can undo everything you did? Mark?"

She didn't give an inch. "When I know we are clear with a five day head start."

Trevor looked at this magnificent creature.

She looked at her watch. "Seth's life goes public in one hour and forty-two minutes. I stop the send or not. And since you don't know where my computer is, just understand that I knew his name is Seth, he rooms with Greg and he's a political science major."

"You're going to pay for this."

"I already did. To the tune of over six figures several times over. Walk away now or lose, because you can't beat me."

She was fearless, standing up to this asshole that lived on intimidation.

"You can buy boy-toys a hell of a lot cheaper than this."

"I'll look into that. Thanks for the recommendation."

"You're planning on fucking them?"

"Every chance I get," she grinned.

"Dibs," Trevor whispered.

Gavin chuckled.

The keys dropped on the ground in front of her, the guards piled back into the van and she checked her watch.

She stepped toward the van absently as it pulled away. When it disappeared he saw her shoulders sag and the huge breath shoot out from puffed cheeks, exhaled through pursed lips. She did have nerves.

She turned back to them in the dark.

The three of them stared off.

"Six figures?" Trevor asked.

"Several times over?" Gavin added.

"You're both kinda cute," she smirked.

She reached over, picked the keys and unlocked their hands from the chain around their waist first, then their feet.

She extended her hand. "My name is Hannah. Hannah Parker."

"I was going with Wonder Woman," Trevor said, taking the hand. Soft, warm and tough as nails. Even their lawyers had stopped this kind of courtesy years ago. "You just single-handedly, without a gun, broke us out of prison?"

She blinked at him. "Do you want to go back? I mean, I was assuming—"

He grabbed her, yanking her forward, planting a hot kiss on her lips and holding her tight.

She backed away with a soft chuckle and looked at Gavin.

"You?"

"I'm good," he smiled.

"Orange is not your color. There are some jeans and shirts in the trunk that might be more comfortable, if you want. The trunk is unlocked if you hurry."

Neither moved.

She looked at her watch again. "Have to take care of Seth."

"That wasn't bullshit?"

She smiled, walking to the car, opened the back door to play on the laptop he saw through the window.

She turned her back on them, he noticed. What had they done to deserve that sign of trust?

"Done," she said, standing back and closing the door.

"You want to explain what the fuck is going on and how the hell you got six figures?"

"First off, I'm not really fond of swearing and don't see the purpose if you would like to think about that. Second, I have many sets of six figures. I inherited them. How I choose to spend them is my business."

"Not when it fucking involves us."

She looked at Gavin and then at Trevor. "Your circumstances weren't fair. I'm not saying I approve of what you did, but I can understand it and when I find two jurors got the first shooters off with no penalty for their crime, I am going to get annoyed. I don't think it's very nice you got convicted when they walked."

"How could you know that?"

She smiled, pointing at Gavin. "Would you like your social first or his?"

"Okay, we get it. You can use a computer, apparently pretty well. How do you know all this?"

"I read all the transcripts. I read transcripts you don't want to know about. I attended most of your trial and I interviewed everyone I could. Juror #4 and juror #12 in the first trial were paid $25,000 apiece. I took the info to the proper channels and no one wanted to help. Apparently vigilantes are more wicked than drug dealers. So I helped myself. Would you like to get going or stand out here more and discuss this?"

They looked at each other.

"She's kinda cute and has millions," Gavin said.

"She just ripped hard-ass prison guards to shreds. What the hell will she do to us?"

"Don't make me angry," she smiled.

"I'm sure that won't be a problem," Trevor grinned.

"I have a house about six hours from here, very secluded with a fully stocked kitchen, showers and six bedrooms. You'll be able to take your pick. I prefer classic rock when I drive, the *Beach Boys* are great for keeping you awake and I will be doing the driving as you have no license yet and there is that little fact you just escaped from prison. So if you could get changed, I would like to get going."

"What if I want your bedroom? What if I insist on it?" Trevor stared at her.

"That can go two ways," she blinked at him. "You go and take it and I will take one of the others, I'm really not possessive. Or you have six hours to convince me why it would be in my best interest to take that offer."

"Maybe I'm that good," he smiled.

"I'm sure you think you are. We'll wait and see if we get a second opinion."

Bribe this person, bribe the next person and keep going up the chain, the payments getting larger until there was no turning back for anyone.

Hannah wasn't going to get caught. Not with the brain God gave her, the money Gr'ma Maureen left or the computers that sat on everyone's desk.

Password protected, my butt.

Here and now, she couldn't help feel maybe she just did the best thing in her life.

The press called them *The Lost Boys*.

Sons born to identical twin mothers, Trevor was ahead by a year. Dark to Gavin's light skin, blue eyes to brown, both boys looked like the fathers they hadn't seen in over two decades.

Payday Morgan, bastard extraordinaire, had sent the assassin team to the wrong house for a deal gone bad. It had taken almost a year after the boys had buried their lost family to have all the people responsible arrested and set for trial. Between the planners, the lookouts and the executioners, there were six total.

All six were acquitted with a jury that had been bought.

With no justice for the victims and all avenues for fairness gone, the boys hunted the six down systematically and killed every one of them.

And when they were done, they stopped running and waited for the law to catch up with them.

She didn't support the death penalty, and after what had been done to them, the horror and grief that edged every facet of their lives, she knew their future had died with everyone they loved.

"Do we scare you?" Gavin asked when he came forward.

She had her arms folded and brought her mind back from the images of reports and crime scenes–she had seen their family in color—and for over two years, unknown to them, their fight was hers.

Until she won.

Because she never lost.

"Not at all."

"You know who we are and what we did?"

She looked at him as Trevor came forward tucking in his shirt.

"You got a woman her inhaler."

"What?" Gavin asked.

"Juror #8 went into trouble and it was the two of you in a roomful of a hundred people who noticed. I noticed because I wasn't listening to the lawyers. I was studying the two of you. So if you ask me if you scare me or I know who you are, I know exactly who you are and it doesn't really involve six bullets."

"She was having an asthma attack."

"I know. And your sister, Emily, had asthma so you noticed, got the bailiff, stopped the days preceding and got on everyone's bad boy list while you helped her."

"I think I'm afraid to find how much you know about us."

"You mean besides the sizes?" Gavin asked.

"Sizes?" she laughed. "Those took about two minutes."

"You don't want to know which one of us pulled which trigger? Seemed to be a question of interest and since we never said we both got stuck with all six."

She turned to look at him. "A lot of loyalty in that statement, don't you think?"

Trevor looked at Gavin then back at her. "That's actually not what my lawyer said."

"Yeah, I know," she said. "You were offered a drastically reduced sentence to turn Gavin in. And Gavin, shockingly, was offered a drastically reduced sentence to set you up for life. Did either of you ever think, even for half a second, to take that offer and walk fifteen years earlier?"

They didn't even look at each other. Neither did they respond to her which was fine. She knew the answer before she asked.

"And both of you thought that van was the death penalty come back to the great state of New Jersey."

Trevor narrowed his eyes at her. "The van had me a little worried."

She turned to walk to the driver's seat. "It was the only way I could walk you out. Sorry for the scare."

"How much?"

She turned to look at him.

"How much did you spend to get us out?" Gavin asked.

She smiled. "I'll have to use coupons for a little while. Thought maybe I wouldn't celebrate Christmas this year, but I live alone so what am I missing?"

"Come on," Gavin said. "Everyone celebrates Christmas."

Her smile broadened. "I'll just have to wrap the two of you in ribbon and set you under the tree."

Gavin's head snapped toward Trevor with a laugh. "I'm not touching that one."

"I'll touch it."

She pulled her purse from the passenger seat and got a lip balm, putting some on.

She smiled, really feeling it. There was a strange sense of coming home when they had so far to go.

"I set out two ham and cheese sandwiches on sourdough on the hood. There's a bag of chips and some Snapple lemonades. The Oreos are optional."

They had been inside 852 days, living on institution food and their expression bordered on awe.

The way they moved, made her smile. Trevor grabbed the lemonade, took off the lid and drank it down to half in one shot. Then he read the trivia on the inside of the top. Gavin went for the cookies first.

"You do realize that seven hours ago your life, though very unpleasant, was predictable. You do understand what I just did. You are escaped convicts and your life will never be the same."

Trevor stood straight and looked at her. "Where we goin'?"

CHAPTER TWO

Several times over. That's what she said. She had spent several times over, Trevor thought as he came down the main stairs to the posh living room decorated in leather, art and money. The car was expensive. The house she pulled in front of in upstate New York in the early hours of the morning was enough to make him know they were in over their heads. This house surpassed anything within a hundred mile radius of the Jersey City Street he had been raised on.

Just out of the greatest hot shower he had ever had — there had been no guard — so many razors he shaved twice for the hell of it, not worried in the least about irritation with the soap she had provided. It smelled like spring and didn't feel like sand paper. His hair wet, his feet bare, he stood at the bottom of the stairs and looked around. He was wearing sweats that felt smooth on his skin, a T-shirt that proclaimed Lynyrd Skynyrd's 'Free Bird' and he didn't think her choice was on accident. All of the clothes, in his style and size, had matched him, making him think she may have known which bedroom would be his.

She paid for their ride, their clothes and everything else that came next.

Not once in his entire life had he let a date pick up the check.

He could smell the scent of something with spice and butter from the kitchen, but he wasn't ready for that yet. He wanted to talk to Gavin and Gavin wasn't in the room he had taken this morning. The clock in Trevor's room said it was close to three in the afternoon.

Moving quietly down the hall, he looked in a few rooms without going in, until he found an office with Gavin behind the computer.

"I swear to God," Trevor said stepping into a two story library. It had a loft above with wrought iron steps going up either side. "We're in a fucking game of Clue. I just passed a billiard room, a dining room and swear there is a conservatory around here somewhere."

"Do you even know what a conservatory is?"

"Yeah, it's in the corner and has the secret passage."

"What are you saying? You like that mattress in the cell better than the one you just slept on? Cuz I slept fine. I slept better than I have slept in a couple of years. Felt pretty damn safe, too."

"Tell me you don't think this is fucked-up?"

"How did you sleep?" Gavin asked with sincere concern. Since it happened sleep was a luxury neither of them visited often.

"Almost six hours," Trevor said.

"Me, too."

"Nightmares?" Trevor asked. Gavin had had them since that day. Trevor's seemed to diminish some, but Gavin was one of those blessed people who remembered his dreams in detail.

Gavin stared at him. "Not as bad last night. It felt good."

"This is still fucked."

Gavin leaned back in the chair and sighed, "Are you denying we're supposed to be somewhere else? You didn't do it?"

"I did it." Gavin said, "I know you did it. I've just never been able to find a place that puts us besides alone on Christmas and I hate being alone at Christmas. I'm not alone now since you're here."

"I want to understand why. There isn't a reason. She isn't anybody to us. She shouldn't be a part of this," Trevor said.

"Maybe we should ask what is on her mind."

Trevor put his arms up and out in frustration. "I was making $10.35 an hour at Home Depot when it went down and I outdid you. What does a house like this even cost?"

Gavin's gaze shifted down to the computer then back up.

"Do you like her?" he asked Trevor.

"I'm not answering that. Not until I know what happened."

"Because you're not going to have to answer that for me. I can tell when you like just fine."

"Fuck you," Trevor said, seeing Gavin smile.

"What are you looking at?" Trevor asked.

Gavin looked back at him. "I would say a great big fuck."

Trevor came closer, walking around the desk. He stared at the computer.

"Ah fuck."

Hannah worked in the kitchen practicing the domestic routine she loved and never got to play at.

The stove hot with the smell of melted butter, she dipped the bread in the mixture and put the French toast on the griddle to brown. Fruit salad with strawberries and blueberries and her special dressing waited on the table. There was orange juice, milk and coffee ready.

They hadn't had a decent meal in too long. Making one for them made her feel good.

Last night in the car, they had sat side by side in the backseat with her compliments. They needed time to get reacquainted.

Glances in the rear view mirror told her they were high fiving, sitting close and aware of each other. They told stories of before, when it was happy. They never talked about the ordeal.

More than once she glanced into that mirror and saw Trevor watching her, his eyes narrowed. He never looked away in embarrassment of being caught and she only watched as long as it was safe for driving.

She knew the dialogue was based on decades of talking in front of people and knowing what each other meant. They were twins without the same mother. They hadn't been rude to the point of using the Spanish she knew they both knew.

Giving them back to each other had been an important element in this project.

Five and a half years ago they had killed six men. Trevor shot three. Gavin shot the others. Only they knew who killed who.
Their mothers—raising them without their fathers—all lived in one household. Trevor and Gavin had been struggling with two jobs each to help finance the house and give their moms a break. The boys got their high school diplomas but they never studied further.

Good people living hand to mouth with enough kids under one roof, to make some days tough. There was a twelve year old sister, an eight year old brother and two kids under the age of five and a baby.

Drug dealers had slaughtered them all while the two men worked a night shift.

Hannah had read everything there was to read concerning the case at least once, usually many more times. Trevor had been at Home Depot, loading stock when his mom was murdered. When the shots had fired, he had been stacking light bulbs in ignorant bliss.

Gavin had been at Wal-Mart doing the same, only it was diapers.

Twenty-three and twenty-two at the time, they dated some, saw only a couple of movies and spent the rest of their time keeping enough money coming in to assist with the rent, food and the little shoes so many kids needed.

And if they had been home, they would have been asleep in their beds too, dead without knowing what hit them.

They were good boys, she thought, checking the French toast.

Now they were good men.

"What's this?" Trevor snapped.

She glanced at the computer printout Trevor held, gave a huff, then went back to French toast.

The letters FBI were a little obvious as was the dollar amount.

"That is a really bad picture of me," she said. She turned to smile at them. "It was my one mistake in a seriously perfect execution," she said transferring the French toast to plates.

"You made a mistake?"

"Yes. I was forced into a meeting with a lawyer in a location I didn't control. He had that photo taken then tried to blackmail me with it."

"You have a fifty thousand dollar bounty on your head?" Trevor asked.

She looked at him and pointed at the name. "Katherine Hill has a fifty thousand dollar bounty and I'm not surprised.

I expected it to show up at some point. I was surprised it took that long."

He looked at the print out again then at her. "Who the hell is Katherine Hill and why does she look just a little bit like you?"

"Ray Bradbury."

"What about him?"

"*Punishment Without Crime*. It's one of his short stories. One I liked. I needed a name, and I went with hers. Thought the title felt right, too."

"You gave yourself up for this cause," Gavin said. "The FBI has a warrant out on you."

"I gave Katherine Hill up," she said, "and I was using that name because I expected it. She has the warrant."

He stared at her. Gavin stared at her.

She turned off the stove, moved the plates to the table then turned to get three matching white mugs, filling each with hot coffee. She looked at them.

"I don't know how you like your coffee. Coffee wasn't on my list of things I needed to know to pull this off, so I never looked."

Trevor worked his jaw. "Black."

"Milk," Gavin said.

She nodded and moved to the refrigerator.

"What about you?" Trevor asked. She turned to look at him.

"What about me?" she asked in complete innocence.

"How do you like *your* coffee?"

The surprise must have registered on her face.

"Oh," she said. "Um, flavored creamers. I usually have French Vanilla but I keep something on hand for special occasions."

He walked to the same refrigerator, looked inside on the door and grabbed a bottle marked Bailey's Irish Crème.

He stopped. "Is this a special occasion?"

"I don't know," she said. "I like the company. I'm usually alone here and this is nice."

He topped off her coffee then got a spoon to stir it lazily in a drawn out silence.

"So what did you do with that lawyer?" Gavin asked. "Anything like what we saw last night with the guards? Were you really going to do all that?"

"I am capable of doing everything I said. Only with great power comes great responsibility," she smiled at her Spiderman reference, but they didn't seem amused. "I can but I wouldn't. It was all threats."

"So you're manipulative?"

"No, just a lot more clever in my execution. The lawyer's name was Curtis Davison. He was an assistant for the prosecution. Greedy bastard, too. And I reminded him he might not want to mess with people who have him out-maneuvered, out-gunned and definitely out-brained."

"I think that scares me." Trevor smiled, tight-lipped.

"I'm on your side, remember?" she said. "After he let me know he had the photo and issued his demands, I created the full 'Hill' bio and posted it to a site where he would find it. Then I let him know he had 1437 parking tickets, I spammed his computer with about 400 different porn sites and I sent two dozen roses to his secretary with a card stating thanks for the weekend, love and kisses. Only I messed that one up, too. They went to his wife."

"So you set up the secretary?"

"Not really. She *was* having an affair with him and I had evidence on that, too. And I am sorry. I played fairly nice with what I was doing. He wanted to go for rough. I won't do that."

"But why are we here? It can't possibly be good for you."

"Breakfast?" she smiled, hoping to get them off their line of questioning.

"Why?"

She licked her lips.

"How much did he want?"

She waited, looking down, knowing it was going to come up. She looked up at Trevor.

"He wanted an even million."

Both their gazes snapped to hers, eyes wide and mouths hanging. "What the fuck were you offering?"

She glared at him with pursed lips.

"You're kidding," he laughed. "Language?"

She continued to stare.

"What, pray tell, were you offering?" Trevor sneered.

"My going rate was a hundred thousand. Two lawyers gave me grief and I had to go to two-fifty."

"What the fu—"

He looked at her.

"What was in the briefcase last night?" Gavin asked.

"Two-fifty. It was my fourth and last payment to the guards that helped pull this off."

"How much fucking money do you have?"

She smiled and then laughed and looked at the two of them.

"34C."

"What?" Gavin gasped.

"I am 5'6", I weigh 147 pounds, my cup size is a 34C and this is my natural hair color, though I don't see proof being offered."

"What?" Gavin gasped again.

"You're asking for personal information. I thought I'd offer an alternative because you have about as much right to financial records as you do to my weight, personal regime and bra size."

"Can you cook?" Gavin asked.

She pointed over her shoulder and smiled. "I made breakfast and it's still warm."

"What about Katherine Hill?" he asked.

Hannah smiled. "Fast food queen. Weighs about three-hundred pounds. You dated her for quite a while, Trevor."

"I was always open-minded," Trevor said.

"Since you broke out by unknown means, you've been traveling down highways 81 & 40. You'll hit 75 soon."

He slammed the creamer onto the counter and she jumped, showing a nervousness she usually hid from strangers.

"None of that happened," he said.

"It did on the computer. Katherine Hill died in a fiery crash yesterday in Richmond. They haven't identified her yet, but they're going to with dental records and her known association with you, she'll be ID'd."

"What?"

"It's not real. Do you understand? It's all smoke and mirrors using computer chips and data. No one is going to visit the crash site, the coroner will not be looking at a real body, but his computer says he did. No one is going to figure it out."

"Why not? We get caught—do you have any idea what happens to us? Escaping is frowned upon and this might be the worse idea ever. And no one asked us."

"I couldn't," she said. "I couldn't go into the visitor rooms. I would have to sign in and our conversations would be recorded. And what would I say? 'I'm breaking you out?'"

"She has a valid point," Gavin said.

"Is it really bad to be here, to be free?" she asked. "You have another chance when you didn't."

"And maybe we'll shoot up the place."

She held onto the counter and bobbed her head, biting her lip.

They didn't want this. There wasn't actually any requirement to them playing house until she could finish and get them set up. Knowing where they were and what they were doing made it easier for her to control the situation, but she could do it without.

"I started sending red roses on all their birthdays and Christmas and Mother's Day. I thought you would like that. You can't go there, though. Not when you leave here. It will be watched and you will be arrested. Do you understand?"

"I think I understand you adopted yourself into our family when no one was looking."

With a sharp but quiet intake of breath, she took a step back and put a hand to her gut. People and her, they were not close knit. She didn't have family she saw, she had few friends who lived in the city. All she really had were her contacts through her job and she wouldn't tell any of them a piece of personal information.

Neither of them said anything.

She looked up at Trevor. "Your new ID is in a bank deposit bag in the drawer by the front door. I kept your first names but Trevor, your new last name is Galban and Gavin, yours is Cadden. There is a Sheffield Bank account already set up with enough in it to get you started wherever you want. There's cash, too, in the bag. You can have the Explorer. The keys are in the drawer, too."

She looked at them.

"Go," she said. "You can start on the run and end up where you want. I can manipulate any searches from here and keep up the flowers. It's no trouble. You will be safe. I promise."

She picked her coffee and went to the table, pouring a glass of milk. Sitting down, she reached for the syrup. She looked at her French toast, added the fruit salad and knew she could enjoy her cooking even if she was doing it alone. She actually knew that fact really well.

"You have really good coffee," Gavin said.

She rested her head in her hand, her elbow on the table. "It's from Germany. I do indulge in some places."

"Some places?" Trevor asked.

She looked up and he was watching her. "Is that your problem? That I broke a few laws to put you in this kitchen or that I have money? Because I have a ton of money that I almost never touch and you know what? Until a couple of years ago, it did me no good except attract people who thought they were entitled. The house is my grandmother's. I inherited from her six years ago and I use four rooms. I had an apartment in the city, but I sold it when I started this. I stay here. Alone. I don't even have a cat."

Gavin moved first, but then Trevor joined him.

"What did she do?" Trevor asked, taking a seat.

"She was good to me. Do you want some breakfast? I have powdered sugar I didn't put out."

Trevor pursed his lips and nodded. "I can't remember the last time I had French toast with powdered sugar."

"Naw," Gavin laughed. "I had it last Tuesday. The cook liked to put it on just about everything."

She smiled and went to a cupboard.

Something had changed. Trevor sat across from her. It looked to him that the level of questions they had presented had turned to rejection in her mind.

He wasn't rejecting her. What she had done was amazing and it looked to be fairly motivated by their interests and not hers.

"Do we have a plan?" he asked as they ate—ate amazing food unlike anything an institution thought of. The French toast melted on his tongue, the salad had fresh fruit. They didn't get all that much fresh fruit and when they did it wasn't strawberries and blueberries.

"I figure we wait here about six weeks," she said. "Things should clear pretty well. We'll set you up in the city of your choice. This house has an indoor pool and a Jacuzzi. They were empty, but I got them up and running for you. There's billiards and a library. There is an entertainment room with a TV. You just have to keep busy."

"What did your Grandmother do?"

She looked up. "Art. A lot. She was an artist as well as a collector. There is a pretty nice studio above the garage with a great view of the grounds. Her office is off that. Her art supplies are old, but I can get new if that's an interest, only please don't move her work that is still up there. I have it like I want it. My grandfather died eight years ago. He was into a lot of stuff. They did well." "

"How well?"

She looked at the table and he could see the intake of breath and the tremor to her hands.

"Will you continue to judge me on something I had nothing to do with?"

"We're not used to it," Gavin said.

"I've had money my whole life," she said. "And any happiness I ever got was from ignoring it and not using it. I keep a solid job that pays well and I live off that. I never really touched the principal until I needed it to balance the circumstances I thought was wrong. Then all of a sudden it was damn useful. I think you are enjoying the perks of that."

"Can you tell me why you did it, really did it?"

"I don't know, really. I knew I was in the right place and I knew I had to run with it."

"And you understand we're guilty?"

"That would depend on what you are looking at."

"What does that mean?"

"I never focused on the second trial, your trial. I concentrated on the first and the men who did this to you. You were victims then, lost in sorrow, sitting watching them get away with it. You never missed a day of court. I've been to Baywater Cemetery a number of times, knowing you had sat in the exact spot and decided. I met with your legal councils. I sat and had coffee with your friends and Aunt Kira, my condolences, by the way. I liked her. She was very nice."

"Try beaming her in the face with a soapy sponge at the youth car wash," Trevor smiled.

"All that red hair covered in bubbles," Gavin added. "It was beautiful." He chuckled.

"Didn't know she could run that fast."

Gavin batted Trevor on the shoulder back handed. "I didn't know *we* could run that fast."

Hannah smiled.

She looked at Trevor. "Everybody likes you. Do you know that? Everyone who talked to me about the good things the boys did to keep a family going when they were all alive. They said good things about you even after you went away. I liked that. I think that says a lot."

"Why don't you have a cat?" Gavin asked.

She looked down, a move Trevor figured meant she hurt. "I had a cat." Her tilted gaze came to his. "His name was Hudson and he was amazing but he got sick and died. There was nothing anyone could do and not a single dime I had made a difference. Do you understand that concept?"

"I'm sorry. That must have been bad here if you were alone."

"Thank you. I miss him. He was a pain in the butt, but I miss him."

"Why was he a pain?" Trevor asked.

She smiled and looked at him with an angled smile. "He liked to pee on bath towels. It could get on your nerves. It didn't matter where I left them, he always found the buggers and then, if you missed the obvious signs, you had to take two showers to get off what he left."

They smiled.

"You have a job," Gavin asked. "You said you have a job. What is this? Your vacation time?"

"I have an office here. I work from home."

"What do you do?"

She looked at Trevor and pursed her lips.

"That's a hard question?"

"I'm just not sure you're going to like the answer."

"Stripper?" Gavin asked, sipping his coffee and looking innocent. "No," he said perking up and pointing at her. "One of those adult webcams where people pay you to—"

Trevor back handed him on the shoulder.

She smiled, looking pretty. "Independent consultant."

Trevor chuckled. "Avon? Cuz the house screams Avon."

She sighed. "Full/Disclosure. That's my company."

"What does your company disclose?"

"I'm a homicide investigator. All cold case homicides, though I rarely go back further than 20 years."

"What?" they both gasped.

"Yeah, I know. I work with law enforcement agencies all over the country. Always on homicides and while I've been doing that, I've been working in the background getting two men out of jail for something most people like me would turn them in for."

"That's insane."

"It's how I knew what to do and who to contact."

The pause lasted. "You work homicide? Doesn't that you make you a really stupid cop?"

"Stupid isn't actually one of my problems. I wish it was. And no, I am not with law enforcement. I just work with them. I'm a private citizen motivated by personal history. And I turned down the FBI when they asked and the ATF when they asked and I will always turn them down as that's not where my loyalties are."

"That makes no sense."

"The jurors who were paid off, they were sentenced to three years because of what I provided anonymously. All the attorneys who knew? Reports arrived in the right mailboxes. I had to keep me out of it or they might track this plan."

"How smart are you?" Trevor asked, deadpan.

"The second trial?" Gavin asked. "Why wasn't that stopped?"

She smiled. "You were guilty."

Gavin looked at Trevor. "Forgot that detail. "

"Everyone did what they were supposed to in prosecuting you," she said. "Except you two really didn't cover your tracks well at all. You made their case. Can't help you on that one. Had neither one of you heard the term 'trace evidence'?"

"Payday," Trevor said.

She kept her gaze up. "He went to South America."

"We heard that, too. Even inside. Everyone liked to remind us. Never heard what happened."

"Piña Colada?" she offered.

He glared at her. "You know what that man did?"

"Maybe he went fishing," she said.

"You didn't find him. The one guy we missed who was responsible for everything."

She looked at the table. "Answers are usually one step back or two steps forward. The here is rarely where we land."

"That strangely made sense," Gavin said.

"I was in my last year at Vassar getting my Masters in Media Studies. I was just too close to twenty. There was this girl, Karen. I had known her the whole time I was in school. She came to class one day, and then she didn't and it took three weeks for her body to be found. Police tried, they really did, but they couldn't figure it out. So I broke into the computers, evaluated the evidence, found what they missed. When I confessed to what I had done and how, I was hired for more cases before I even applied back to school for another degree in criminology. I found I have a real problem with victims who go unheard."

"Victims like we left?" Trevor asked.

"Victims like you and yours became. I couldn't stop your trial, so I did what I could to make it right."

Gavin looked at Trevor. "That actually sounds like a damn valid reason."

Trevor nodded. "Still has holes."

"I was going to make fried chicken and mashed potatoes for dinner. And I picked up an apple pie at this amazing bakery in town. We have whipped cream and ice cream."

Trevor chuckled with Gavin. "Not fighting fair, huh?"

"You're not afraid of us?"

She looked at Gavin. "Did you see the entertainment room?"

"I didn't go in but I saw it."

"In the closet of that room are two identical boxes. Davison got them for me. One for each of you. They have everything you had on you when you were arrested. Clothes, watches, I guess photos. I actually never went through them as they weren't mine. But each box has a 9mm with a suppressor, both with almost full clips. That I did check because I hate guns."

"That's impossible," Gavin said.

"We didn't have the guns on us when we were arrested."

"But you left them with Carl Poole. I bought them from him for ten thousand. He needed the money. Am I afraid of you? You can keep asking and I can keep telling you no. Eventually one of us will give up."

CHAPTER THREE

Prison was predictable: up by five, work by seven, colors drab, clothes in orange. Their schedule didn't vary much day to day. The first few years had some excitement: the trial, the lawyers jostling them around, standing as the verdict was read, separating them forever.

She was there that day. Gavin was led out of the courtroom in shackles first, looking over his shoulder past the guards, gaze locked on the brother he would never see again.

If she could have stopped any of that then, she would have.

Here at home, they still got up early, she knew. She could hear them in the back of her mind as she stayed in her dark room under her quilt and kept her same schedule of rise and shine at 10:30 am.

They waited on breakfast until she came down, the food cooked, the table set.

"Thanks," she said, when Trevor sat her coffee in her spot, pouring in her creamer to make the brew the color she liked.

Settling into a routine, they amused her.

Gaming systems. Netflix. ESPN. They *loved* ESPN. The real fun was seeing them with the everyday chores she took for granted and they took as heaven.

Washing the dishes: Trevor stood at the sink, his hands submerged, ignoring the dishwasher. "Hated dishes," he said. "Never appreciated how these bubbles feel."

Laundry: she caught Gavin using two capfuls of the fabric softener.

"Here," he smiled, taking her clothes. "I can throw them in with mine."

When she went to sleep that night, the clothes were folded on her dresser.

They loved to vacuum when it didn't need vacuuming. Lint didn't stand a chance on the dark carpet.

When they ran out of things to do, they took to the yard, racking, shoveling, doing things she never thought needed doing. They dug holes for fun. The swimming pool room that had been closed, now shined with the smell of the chlorine hanging in the air instead of the mildew.

"We were going to watch *Raiders of the Lost Ark*. Do you want to watch with us?" Trevor asked, as she stood up from breakfast to go to work.

She smiled and thanked them, disappearing.

They liked to talk about their family, each member by name. She liked to listen to their stories of Jayce eating a snail when he was little or Emily trying to sneak out past her Mom covered in make-up. They laughed. They got teary.

"One movie, Hannah?" Trevor asked every morning.

She always declined.

They never excluded her from anything.

She withdrew because she thought they needed more time and because she didn't know what to say. Alone was her norm and men were not her specialty. Keeping a few steps between the two worlds of them here and them gone, it would make it easier for everyone later.

Tuesday morning they small-talked through breakfast and she kept up with the current events.

They were both in their trunks this morning: Trevor blue and Gavin red. Towels on their necks, no shirts. The builds on both said they did some sort of working out even in prison. One had blonde hair on his chest, the other, smooth. She tried not to stare at the tattoos they carried though the ink fascinated her. Men she had dated in the past thought they were too sophisticated for tattoos though sneaking a peak at Trevor and Gavin, she was beginning to think those morons before could improve their sexy look by taking a lesson from these two.

"I'll have lunch ready about 1:30?" she offered, standing to clear her place.

"Make it something good this time, woman," Trevor said, straight-faced.

She stopped halfway to the sink, turned slowly and raised her chin in defiance at him. "Excuse me?"

His smile broke his face. "I was just saying I look forward to it. Your lunches are always great."

"Ah huh," she put her plate in the sink, picked up her coffee and turned towards the hall, got to her office then walked to the free floating desk facing the room and the door.

"What are you working on?"

Her gaze came up as she sat her coffee on her coaster, more than surprised Trevor had followed her. She stood straight.

"I thought you were going swimming? I mean you look like you are going swimming."

He looked down at his suit then back at her. The towel still around his neck matched his eyes and she didn't want to notice that.

"Can I come in?" he asked.

"Sure," she sat, adjusting her seat.

"That office down the hall? Two story library? Wrought iron, curved stairs. Not bad."

"It was my grandfather's. This one suits me."

He looked side to side at the dark wood furniture. The art on the wall was original and expensive, though for her it came cheap. They were by Gr'ma M. She leaned back on the leather.

"It's nice." He sat in the chair across from her.

"Do you need something?" she asked.

"Just wanted to see what you were doing. You always disappear when we start something."

"It's called a job," she smiled. Her gaze ticked down to her desktop on the computer, seeing the 'payday' icon in the lower right corner. Trevor was right in her office, staring with that smile and all she had to do was print to pass the info on. He needed to know. She had to tell him. Sometime.

And right now that smile would be gone and she wasn't sure it would be back.

"What job are you working on now?" he asked.

She picked up her coffee and took a sip. "A cold case."

"All your cases are cold cases. Is it classified?"

She shook her head. "I'm not used to discussing them with someone without credentials."

He leaned back, thought, then smiled. "I did 852 days of detailed research into the prison system and how it deals with people who commit heinous crimes."

"Get many dates that way?"

He sat forward to brace his elbows on his knees. "No, but there was this guy, Raul. He was making pretty impressive offers. I was waiting to see how high he went."

She chuckled. "What was he offering?"

"Chocolate mostly. Didn't do much for me. I'm more of a caramel person."

She tilted her chin. "Are you going to go away and let me work?"

"Not likely."

His hair was dark, hanging longer than she usually liked on a man. She liked it on him fine. She liked the black onyx in his left ear lobe. There was a quality about him stating confidence lined with buried grief. It didn't feel right to say no to him.

"Sixteen-year old murder for a sixteen-year old girl. Kansas."

"Is she missing?"

"Yes. He buried her too deep."

"Is that what drives you? Stopping them?"

She leaned back, wondering if this was a conversation she should have. She wasn't under any oath not to talk. She never had because there was no one to tell.

"Chances are if someone got away with it once, they may have figured out how to do it again."

"Which you knew we wouldn't so we got a pass on your radar."

She stared at him and he was staring back, totally relaxed. "Is that what's bothering you?"

He shook his head. "I'm not bothered. I'm curious. You are either completely trying to avoid us while doing everything you can to make us comfortable, or you are totally obsessed with your work."

"How about both?"

"Was the plan to ignore us when you brought us here?"

She stared at her desk. "I'm not ignoring you. I just—I'm not used to people. Especially here, in this house. Retreat seems like the best course for me. No attachments when you go."

He nodded, looking serious. "Come swimming with us."

She laughed, reaching for the lip balm on her desk, putting some on. She pointed at the tattoo on his chest. It wasn't big, just a few inches, but it was colorful, located on his right pec. "What's that for?"

He glanced down, then back up. The smile made the eyes sparkle more.

"Corvette. The first car we bought, tore down, rebuilt and sold was a Corvette." He looked around. "Made enough on it to buy at least one of the vases around here."

She pointed at his bicep with the geometric patterned armband in deep, dark ink.

He looked at that one, too. "I was twenty. Thought it looked cool. Still like it."

"That's good. I think you're stuck with it."

"Do you have any?" he asked with genuine interest.

"No," she smiled. "Never seemed to go with me, the lifestyle or the company I kept."

"You have new company and I think I can think something for you."

She knew he had another tattoo taking up the majority of his back. A crossbeam across his shoulder blades, the staff dipped to his waist. Seven roses, one for each member lost, vined around the staff of the cross. The word Faith and Family sat on either side on the top vertical bar. Gavin had the exact same tattoo only his roses were a mirror image to Trevor's, his words reading Family and Faith.

This morning she had seen glimpses of the art while they had breakfast in their trunks, but she hadn't stared.

She knew about those tat's because there was a photo in each of their prison files.

He stared at her.

"Let me ask you a question." She smiled, leaning back.

"Anything."

"Have the two of you ever competed for the same girl?"

He laughed and looked away. "I like your terminology."

"Is that a yes or a no?"

"Yes," he looked at her.

She blinked at him.

"She was a blonde. Big green eyes. She had both of us wrapped around whatever she wanted to wrap us around. Her name was Cindy and she was in the 7th grade; Gavin was in 8th and I was in 9th She was way too young for us but she gave us half her Twinkie."

"Same Twinkie?"

He shook his head. "Two different lunch hours."

He smiled at her.

"I was serious."

"I am serious. We got into fights cuz of her. One night, right after dusk we were in the backyard going at it, vowing to destroy each other. Mom came out with a big bucket of water and nailed both of us. Told us to get a grip. It didn't stop us and we swore we would hate each other forever. Or at least until first period the next day because by then Cindy had hooked up with Mark Altman and we decided he deserved her."

"That's a tragic story."

"I know, isn't it?"

"Now?"

He pursed his lips and shrugged a shoulder. "No need. Totally different tastes. I gave up blondes after Cindy while he liked the flavor. He likes that whole pale look with light eyes. I think it looks washed out. I like brunettes. Brown eyes, thick hair. Not too skinny."

"Thank you."

"I didn't say anything to be worried about. I just prefer curves. What do you like?"

"What?" She laughed at the absurdity of the question.

He stared at her.

She laughed a little. "If I had to pick a quality I look for, I would start with dressed."

He looked to the side and laughed. He looked back at her. "Come swimming with us."

"I have a project due."

"It's a cold case, Hannah. Sixteen-years old. I bet it can wait a few hours."

Sitting on the edge of her desk, contrary to everything pristine, sat a little guy, his fur orange, the grin dumb. Only eight inches high, he had a hard plastic area on his stomach with fluid that seemed to move even when he didn't.

His name was Future Frank and in a house of antiques so valuable museums drooled, he was one of her prized possessions.

She smiled at Trevor and reached for the stuffed toy, shaking it a bit. *"Do I think I will go swimming anytime soon?"* she smiled. Pulling the little orange guy next to her, she read the space in his stomach that gave the answers.

"Maybe yes, maybe no," she brought her gaze to his.

"Those guys have been known to make mistakes. The one I had as a kid fucked all the time."

She tossed the doll to him. He caught it over hand. "Stop swearing and he is always on my desk and I always ask."

"You're getting advice from a good source."

"One more," she said, leaning forward. "*Will my next check arrive here, or should I notify the right people to have it forwarded?*"

He stared at her crooked.

"What's it say?" she asked.

He shook Future Frank in his hand and looked for the response.

"*Everything is in order,*" he said, looking at her.

She smiled. She pointed at the doll and he looked at it. "Trevor, that is one of the first Franks to come off the line. One of the first ten, actually. If I posted that on eBay, the amount of money I could make would make one of these vases look like Play Dough."

"I'm sure my Mom had mine somewhere. What are we talking about?"

"Trevor, my grandfather invented Future Frank."

He looked at her, looked at the doll in his hand and then back up.

"That number you've been trying to put an estimate on, it's worse than you think. Future Frank was making mega millions at his debut twenty years ago. You can still buy him at Target today, meaning he is still making me mega millions. I talked to people who knew you and I've seen you scoff at the stuff in this house. Money and you don't like each other. I'm thinking you probably aren't so interested in what kind of bathing suit I own now."

He nodded his head, pursed his lips and stood up to lean over the opposite side of the desk, placing Future Frank in his position on the wood.

"You know what," he said. "I've never liked bikinis. No imagination required. I like a nice one-piece. Solid color. Nothing to break up the lines. Do you back-up your computer?"

"About fifty times a day."

"That sounds smart." His arm jerked, she felt the tug in the desk and every aspect of her system went down from screen to printer to the land line phone she kept for faxes.

Tilting her chin, feeling a little bit more than irritation, she looked at him, who still held the cord.

"Power outages," he smiled. "You never know when but they do give you a day off on occasion."

CHAPTER FOUR

Waiting in the kitchen for her, feeling only mildly guilty, he spent more time staring at the cupcakes she baked and decorated last night than most would deem appropriate. He had watched strippers with less interest than he was watching the chocolate cake with white frosting and sprinkles. Where the hell had she found little tiny sugar handcuffs, he couldn't even imagine. They tasted pretty good, though.

Two cakes sat naked of their iron and he licked his lips.

He picked at one cupcake, grabbing little bits without making too much damage. Mom had always said you had to wait for the cookies until everyone was home.

Never stopped him when Mom's back was turned. He had the paper pulled off and had half the cake in his mouth when she stepped into the room with those doe eyes eyeing him as he chewed.

"Was making sure you got it right," he smiled.

"How did I do?" That twinkle in her eyes said flirt, not busted.

"If you get tired of solving crimes you could probably get a job at a bakery."

Nodding, he tossed the rest back. He was trying hard not to be too blatant about checking her out but the extremely modest black one-piece under the extremely modest sheer black cover almost killed him. Glancing down, before turning to wipe his crumbs, he thought maybe it was the red toe nail polish that might do him in.

He put a hand on the small of her back and directed her toward the indoor pool. He and Gavin had opened the massive windows on the south side about ten minutes after they found the room. Sweet July air, smelling of pine and forest blew in, changing the mood from lock down to acceptable.

"Hey, Gavin?" he shouted as they cleared the door.

The pool room may rival some hotels, though not huge. The floors were stone tiles in deep rust, the water blue. The pool was oval with enough room for a deep-end and few stairs in the shallow to offer entrance. The square Jacuzzi on the opposite side was hot now that they had found the controls and pool cleaning had come up under Things to Do.

Gavin was examining a raft like it was science. "What?" he shouted back without looking up.

"I found out how she does it."

"I guess that depends on what she does and do I want to know."

"Gr'pa Ernest invented Future Frank. Our future is worse than you know."

Gavin stood straight. "No shitting?" he laughed. "I had one of those."

"Judging by the digs, I think a lot of people had one of those."

"Hey," she scolded, dropping her towel on a chair and pulling off the wrap. "Language."

"Yeah," Trevor laughed. "You keep working on that one and we'll catch up."

The toys they had for the pool were limited. A few from a by-gone era had been found in the wooden chest. The rest consisted of sponges from the kitchen, filled water bottles, a bucket. There had been a couple of rafts they inflated.

"All we had in the neighborhood growing up was a YMCA in the summer."

"I never ever came down here," she sighed.

"Never?"

She floated face down on the yellow raft. Good color for her, he thought then mentally slapped himself.

"Gr'ma M had arthritis. She used to keep the Jacuzzi heated high and then I would do one with her but that was about it." She raised her head a little. "I had a friend in high school come for a week once. Brooke Adams. She was cool. We hung out in here."

"Where is Brook Adams now?"

"Paris. She got a position at the embassy then met a French guy."

"I assume she had to speak French?"

Hannah raised her head and smiled. "*Qui.*"

She fell back onto the floating mattress looking sexy and giggling a little.

"I bet you speak a couple," Gavin said, floating face up on the green.

"A couple," she mumbled into the rubber.

"Spill 'em." Trevor said.

She turned her head to the side, pursed her lips with a smile. "*Je parle français.*"

He didn't know what had him smiling more. The fact she said it or the fact the accent was dead on.

"*Yo hablo español. Ich spreche Deutsch. Ya govoryu po-Russkiy.*"

"I'm not sure what you said but I think the last part of it was in Russian."

She smiled more and hid her face.

Brown eyes, brown hair and beautiful curves. He was focusing on the conversation fine.

"Is that it?" Gavin laughed.

"*Italiano. Japanese et Klingon.*"

"Klingon. You are telling us, with a straight face, you speak Klingon?"

"I was bored."

"Prove it."

"*LupDujHomwIj luteb gharghmey.*"

Trevor grinned. "What the hell does that mean?"

"My hovercraft is full of eels."

"Yeah," he laughed. "I see where that one is handy."

Gavin laughed, too. "I lost count. Do I want to know?"

She screwed up her face and shook her head.

"School?" Trevor asked.

"Naw. I used to get bored a lot."

Two hours later, probably still too early in the afternoon for indulging, they each had a beer enjoying the Jacuzzi, in bubbly heaven, the heat set high.

"You never use this?" Gavin asked her.

"No," she said. "I always thought it was a little risky for me to be in the water. No one ever calls except for work, so I could be gone for a long time before anyone noticed."

She took a long drink.

"That's a lot of time alone," Trevor sighed.

She smiled a little and shrugged. "Gr'pa was here until eight years ago, and then Gr'ma M was six. Hudson went to sleep three months ago."

"What about your folks?"

"What about them?"

"You don't like to talk about your folks? Are they dead or something?"

She looked at Gavin. "Or something."

Feeling the mood shift down, Trevor floated closer to her while she stared at him. "I think you should at least get another cat."

She laughed a little. "I thought about it. But it was hard losing him, watching that. He got real sick. I don't think I'm ready."

"Two cats," Gavin said, smiling goofy.

"What about two cats?"

"She should get two kittens. Boys. Name one 'G' and one 'T' then no matter where she sends us, she's got us here."

She smiled and drank the beer.

"Can you take the rest of the day off?" Trevor asked. "It gets boring with him all the time."

She smiled at him. "Yeah, because it looks like you're suffering."

"Tried to amuse myself with some of these puzzle books…"

Her gaze darted to his.

"Crosswords, Sudoku, word searches. Can't find any that haven't been completely filled in with blue pen with no errors."

"Gr'pa left those."

"Yeah, sure. You do your crossword in ink with no errors?"

"How do you do yours?" she smiled.

He stared at her. "It was eight, Gavin. I did count. If you count English, she speaks eight languages."

She took a drink off her beer. "I do speak English," she smiled.

The plan had never been to care too much. She knew some attachments might form and Christmas cards would be exchanged. But real affection? No. That wasn't planned for and planning is what she did best.

"Sixteen-year old case?" Trevor asked, his second beer in hand.

"What about it?"

"Are you close?" Gavin asked.

She took a drink, pursed her lips, debated then smiled. "I finished it last night, but I didn't type up the report yet. I wanted to make the cupcakes."

"How did you find sugar handcuffs?"

"Online specialty shop. They had other interesting things but I didn't think they'd be appropriate."

"Like what?"

"Penises. They had little purple penises."

She took a drink, and tried not to smile as the two hardened convicts got embarrassed. The point was her victory. She couldn't help but smile.

"Not really into eating penis regardless of my recent residence, but a boob would have been nice," Trevor volleyed back.

"Yeah," Gavin smiled and laughed. He pointed at Trevor with his bottle. "That would be good. "

She set her drink down, and turned back toward them, using her hands to demonstrate in the most elaborate fashion. She made circles. "You can't get the whole shebang, because well, the cupcake *is* the boob. But you can get these little edible tops that…"

"Edible?" Gavin laughed.

"Yes, of course." She used her hand to mimic the cupcake and placing an object on top. "You frost the cake kinda pink and then you place the—"

Trevor moved closer to put his hand on her mouth.

"Who did it?" he laughed.

She pulled his hand, laughing at how uncomfortable they both looked.

"Parking attendant."

"How do you know?" Gavin asked and Trevor floated slowly to his place across from her.

"Because he did it," she said, scratching her nose.

They both stared at her. "We're curious," Gavin said.

"Nina. She was sixteen. She was at a football game and went to use the portables during the 2nd quarter and no one ever saw her again."

"That explains the what," Gavin said.

"The how isn't hard when you take it apart. I read through every file they had. The fact there was an eighteen minute discrepancy between his alibi and his reality should have been caught by someone and that will be noted in my report."

"Is that how you busted him?"

She shook her head. "He had signed the funeral book."

"Funeral book?" Gavin asked.

"You know, the guest book for the funeral? Everyone who went, signed it. And he signed her yearbook with way too much."

"Wait, you have these books?"

"I have digital copies of the full books. The books are still in evidence in Kansas."

"So you don't look at the blood stained anything?"

"No, only the reports."

"What did he write in her annual?"

"*By their own beauties; or, if love be blind...*"

"Okay that sounds good. The fact you can recite it verbatim is scary but at least you did it in English. What the hell does it mean?"

"That's Shakespeare. *Romeo and Juliet*. This guy, who has a broken alibi, was a three year 'D' runner in English. I don't think he found *Romeo and Juliet* lying around."

"So that's what did it?"

"Almost."

"You had to find more?"

"I don't stop until I've read every scrap of paper and Post It note. He signed her Facebook Page."

"Wait," Trevor said, looking confused. "You said sixteen years. How does she have a Facebook page?"

"It's not that strange," she said. "A lot of friends and families set them up as a place to gather and leave memories. I always read them in full. He left messages four times saying the same thing four different ways, each one worse. He covered the wording pretty good and they are spaced but if you see it, you can't miss it."

"What did he say?"

She nodded and felt the same disgust at the man she tracked. "'You really should have gone to the prom with me, bitch'. His word, not mine."

"Wow. That is actually really impressive work."

"It took me a whole day to find him after I figured it out. That's part of my package deal, if I can pull it off. Sometimes I can. Sometimes I can't. This one was tricky. He changed his name to his mom's maiden name so there was no way to tie him to the victim or the school. I'll put that in my report, too. Then they can pick him up. My prediction is a confession."

"Why would he confess?"

"Because he's serving three life sentences in Washington State with no possibility for parole."

"For?"

"Rape and murder, four girls under sixteen."

"Holy fuck. If they had figured out half of that sixteen years ago—"

"One of the perks of the job is knowing that. He's going to try negotiating by offering where her body is, try to get a reduction. I've seen it before. Families are sometimes desperate enough to get the loved one back that they will look the other way when deals are made."

She finished off her beer, her mind clicking, gauging the men. They could handle some of what she hadn't said.

She started to walk to the steps, but on the first, turned to face them. They were mumbling about assholes, then they went quiet, staring at her.

"I don't know if you want to know," she said.

"Know what?" Gavin asked.

She paused with a deep breath. "Janice Hampton?" she said softly.

Trevor's chin snapped up, his stare on hers. His jaw hung agape, his eyes wide.

"What about Janice?"

"I met her. Spoke to her awhile. We had coffee. She had a lot of regrets but she was nice."

"I haven't seen Janice in years."

"I know."

"You met her?" Trevor asked.

She tilted her chin before looking at them. They both stared, waiting.

"Janice set up a Facebook page for your family about four years ago."

"What?" they both said.

"She did a really good job. A lot of photos and messages. Both of you with your family and that Corvette. There is nothing negative on the wall. It's a place to celebrate your family. Even people who only know the story and not the people have left messages. If you want to see it. You can use my account."

Morning found him tired not only from the all night Facebook reading, but the things he saw and he read. Faces of people lost to him put together by a woman he had briefly known. People left comments. People they knew. People who knew the cases. There was no judgment. He was slow this morning coming downstairs to breakfast, confused by the entry he found in the pages from two years ago:

Hannah Parker

"We usually lose today, because there has been a yesterday, and tomorrow is coming." ~Johann Wolfgang von Goeth. *Hold on. Help is on the way.*

That simple message meaning more to her at the time than them, proved she was already planning their new lives years before he got here.

He liked her. He liked the look of her, the smell of her though he couldn't place the perfume. She laughed at the funny stories they came up with and she was sincere.

Walking into the kitchen, though in his experience kitchens were six feet wide, Gavin sat at the counter, a bowl, a spoon, a banana peel at his side. He had the TV Guide open.

Comfortable in silence, neither said a word while Trevor got his frozen waffle out of the freezer and popped it in the toaster, then turned for his coffee from the massive espresso coffee magic maker.

He had stopped thinking about its origin and how many small children had been used to build it.

Every room had indication that screamed wealth all based on eight inches of orange fur. How twisted was that, he thought. She never flaunted it, but he knew Future Frank paid the bills.

"Mets are playing Boston later. If you're interested."

Trevor turned toward him. Gavin's gaze was on the *TV Guide*.

"That sounds good."

"Do you have any other plans for the day?" Gavin asked.

Trevor sipped the coffee. Coffee was damn good here.

"About what?" he asked.

Gavin's gaze went back to the rag. "Been here eighteen days."

"Twenty-one," Trevor said.

"Is it twenty-one? I hadn't realized." Gavin smiled, pissing Trevor off at the trap.

"You have a reason for being a dick?"

"Come on," Gavin said. "Twenty-one days. Either move on it or let someone else in the line."

Trevor pursed his lips a little, nodded his chin and thought long and hard on a couple of things.

1) how he would kick Gavin's ass when Gavin wasn't expecting it.

2) how he would kick Gavin's ass when Gavin wasn't expecting it.

He brought his gaze up to Gavin's.

"She's hot," Gavin said. "Generous to a point I can't even measure and her laugh alone could melt a stadium of men locked up too long."

"You think screwing our benefactor would be appropriate as what? A way to say thank you? I'm thinking if you try that, I might have to interfere."

Gavin rinsed his bowl then turned to stand directly in front of Trevor, in his face.

"I know when you got your first kiss, your first job and the first time you got laid. Actually there aren't many emotions you can pull past me that I won't nail. What you feel for her has nothing to do with sex. You were hooked before the van she got you out of pulled out of that clearing. Tell me I'm wrong."

Trevor put a hand on Gavin's chest and pushed him away. Gavin didn't go far.

"Everything you are thinking and feeling is reciprocated if you weren't too stupid to realize it."

"You have any suggestions to change our circumstances?"

"I'm an outsider, watching in and I can see it. You don't want it to be bothering you but it is. You are so fucking afraid of Future Frank you are frozen in time and space."

"I don't like money."

"She never offered it, mentions it to us and never flaunts it."

Trevor pointed over his shoulder. "That coffee maker is a couple of thousand alone."

"That coffee maker is thirteen years old. I asked. Her Gr'ma liked excess and bought it. Her Gr'ma had high taste.

Hannah sits in ten thousand square feet alone because she doesn't have anywhere else to go."

Trevor looked over at the offending machine.

"Trevor," Gavin said, going formal. "I will gladly ask for more of her time. I haven't had a date recently either and she's awesome, but she's not ever going to look at me the way she looks at you."

"Woke up a prick today?"

"No. Loyalties are shifting and I saw her go to bed sad last night after she tried to sit by you and you moved. You don't want what wants you, back the fuck off and stop giving mixed messages. You didn't mind your hands on her in the pool and then she leans toward you, you shut her down?"

Trevor moved to the table with his coffee, ignored the cold Eggo and sat down. He looked up at Gavin.

"Since I didn't think anything could come of being next to her last night with you on the couch, I went to the seat with the best view. I could see her."

"And it hurt her. For some reason, something as little as that hurt her."

"Which explains the pictures," Trevor said.

"What pictures?"

"You haven't noticed? There's no pictures."

"There's pictures in every room," Gavin said.

"No, I don't mean paintings. I mean *pictures*. Of her birthday parties, her family. Mom and Aunt Lucy practically wallpapered our house with all of us, but there is nothing here. Not even albums. You're going to tell me she hasn't been to Europe a few times, seen the Eiffel Tower?"

"Could be on a computer."

"And the way she talks to us?" Trevor said.

"I like it," Gavin said.

"But don't you remember?" Trevor said. "When ours were gone, everyone we knew never mentioned them. They talked of cars or weather or baseball scores. They didn't even bring up the trial because they didn't want us to remember. When Hannah listens she is listening, eyes wide, taking it all in. She understands we don't need reminding because we never forget."

"I've talked to her a few times when you weren't around. I get the feeling she's been hurt in ways we can't imagine. And I think I've kinda become protective of her."

"I like her," Trevor said.

"I know. And you can like her and not want more. Just stop confusing her and back totally off from the romance angle."

"So you can have a chance?"

"So she can have a chance at stability. What we're doing can't be easy on her, either. She works with fucking law enforcement doing a job no one else can while hiding fugitives. Put those words in your head and let them roll around."

He looked at Gavin. "I've never dated anything near her level of sophistication and education. She's fun to hang around with but she's got a couple of degrees, for God's sake. And the languages? I thought our Spanish was good."

"She's never dated anyone like you either. She told me a little but not a lot. I think her taste in guys leans toward professionals and assholes. I think she's nervous about all this."

"Me?"

Gavin nodded. "Talk to her or don't. Hold her hand or don't. Just stop playing it both ways. Pick a direction and commit."

"Are you done?"

"I can be done," Gavin said.

Trevor started walking away without his breakfast then stopped to look at Gavin. "Does it seem at all like home to you?"

Gavin sighed and brought his gaze up direct. "Yes."

Hannah found him on the patio. She had two cups of coffee. He looked up and smiled.

"Hey," he said, closing the book he had been reading, setting it down on the table.

"Do you want company?" she asked, feeling shy. She wasn't playing hard to get but Trevor and Gavin usually came to her to play and not the other way 'round.

"Sure," he said, reaching for the cup she offered. "Thanks for this. I was too lazy to walk inside."

"Is the book that good?"

He looked at it, turning it so she could read the title.

The Motorcycle Diaries.

"Are you enjoying it?" she pulled her lip balm out of her front pocket to use.

He screwed up his face and put the book on the table. "It's okay but reading was never really my thing."

"You don't like to read?"

He shrugged. "Never got into it at school. Afterwards we were always working. Then our other housing; I guess I got into some there. Had a lot of free time and no way to spend it."

He motioned the book toward her. "Have you read it?" he asked.

She raised her eyes and took a sip of her coffee, holding the mug in both hands.

"Have you read all the books in the library?"

Again she didn't answer.

"How smart are you?"

"I read a lot," she smiled, putting her coffee down.

"34C but you won't tell me if I should play chess with you?"

"I hate chess. What do you like to do?"

"Beside learn more about the 34C?" he asked, taking a sip.

She felt herself blush.

"I was thinking more of how I could amuse you two since you cleaned the place twice and the yard looks great."

He paused, looking at his cup. "I was thinking about Janice, actually," He said.

She leaned away and started to stand. "I'm sorry. I'm disturbing you."

"No. Don't go. That Facebook page brought up lot of things I had forgotten."

She sat back down, but stayed on the edge. "Should I not have showed you?"

"We didn't have drug problems or alcohol problems, but we were listed as a problem case because of our background. Instead of abuse treatment, we had to undergo therapy six days a week. Grief, anger management. A bunch of sh—" He smiled, looking down. "I guess it helped. Neither of us are as screwed up as we could have been."

She settled back into the seat.

"Janice and I never had a traditional relationship, I guess. We were only together about three months when it happened. And she did try to stay, but she was only twenty. She couldn't handle it." He looked at Hannah. "I'm not sure what she told you, but I think we parted okay. She was a good kid."

"Would you do it again?"

"Janice?"

"No," she said.

He looked at her, and then laughed. A shrug told her she had caught him off guard. "No," he said, sad. "Not for after the fact. Maybe there was some justice in what we did, but it doesn't feel like it now. I don't regret what I did, only that I did it."

She nodded her head.

"Mess with mine, though, when I have the choice, probably would end similar."

She looked at him.

"No one is ever taking one of mine from me again. Someone threatens Gavin or you and I will strike with deadly force."

"What?" she laughed soft, feeling the need to hide. "I didn't know you were confused."

He smiled at her. "I know my movies. Butch and Sundance had their Etta Place. Now we have ours."

"Etta Place left them to go home. They died without her in Bolivia."

"And why do I get the feeling that wouldn't happen here?"

She looked down, unable to meet his gaze. "You flatter me."

"Good. Cuz I get the feeling not a lot of people do and it's a job that should be done on a regular basis."

She snapped her gaze to him. "What do you enjoy?"

"You've done enough. And I'm not comfortable taking anymore."

She stared at him. He stared back.

"I have a lot of money."

"Kinda figured that out."

"It sits in banks and does no good to anyone."

"Not the point."

She looked away then back. "How about I find a charity. Something like the Helman Church and I try to guess the amount of what you want and instead of helping you, I make a donation to them in that same amount. All that money you could be enjoying will go to a white supremacist, fascist church who thinks evolution is the spawn of Satan."

"I'm sorry. Are you blackmailing me into giving me more shit?"

Her back went straight.

"Stuff," he smiled. He had a pretty smile. She liked it.

"I can double the donations."

He smiled and gave up. "Cars. We like cars."

She pointed at his chest, the tattoo hidden under the blue T-shirt.

"Yep," he said. "We bought trashed American Muscle. It was sort of a part time job because the money helped, but the truth was we loved it. Rebuilt from the tires to the bolts to the paint. The first was this Corvette"—he tapped his chest—"we got it for under a thousand. Took eighteen months but we made enough to pay and meals for a while."

"What's the appeal?"

He smiled and shrugged a little. "Extra money was nice. We needed it. I think, though, we both liked the challenge, you know. Taking this wreck and piecing it back together. You get to the end and it's not junk anymore. It's something to be proud of."

She smiled, thinking about that.

"If you had a beat up car, would the two of you enjoy that?"

"I think it's something we missed."

"Nothing like that kind of satisfaction when you were inside the system? Don't they have auto shops?"

"Gavin worked in building maintenance, I was in laundry. We each made about forty cents an hour."

"You get paid so you can buy all those cigarettes and things." She smiled.

"Actually," he grinned. "We were both smokers before. Smoking is banned inside so we had to give it up."

She was quiet for a long time before reaching over to pick the book while he watched. She held it up toward him.

"I read it when I was eleven. I've read all the books in the house, most a couple of times. Now, I keep my electronic reader current because it can hold so much."

He watched her.

"The first time they tested me I hadn't hit ten, and then they tested me again to verify. It kind of freaks people out so I try real hard to hide it. But it's why I can do what I do."

He learned forward and crossed his arms on the table. "Lemon bars," he said.

"I'm sorry?"

"I love lemon bars. I mean, I can eat a whole tray of them without breaking sweat. I think it's been years since I had one. They weren't on the menu of my last residence."

"If I find a recipe and make some lemon bars do you think you might sit down at the computer with me and help pick out a clunker?"

"I think if you change your mind on the Helman Church, I might do whatever you want."

CHAPTER FIVE

The rumble of what he knew had to be a tow truck pulled him from his bed at dawn. She hadn't mentioned anything wrong with the Explorer so he came out in his bare feet with his sweats and T-shirt on and met Gavin dressed about the same on the stairs.

"Any clue?" Gavin asked.

Trevor sighed and groaned. "Yeah, I might."

Their discussion had been yesterday. He hadn't gotten a chance to talk to Gavin or meet at the designated computer.

And outside, something with a whole lot of dents, without tires and too much rust was being positioned in the garage. She stood to the side, oblivious to them joining her. She was in purple cotton pajamas, looking bedraggled with messed hair and very kissable.

He leaned over her shoulder to talk into her ear. "Did you send the donation?"

She looked at him, Gavin to his right. The smile could light up the dawn.

"I thought I would wait to see how I did."

"What did you do?"

She kept smiling at him. "There's this little one-garage town about forty-five minutes from here. George."

"George?" Trevor asked.

"George called his buddy Robert who has a junk yard and told him what I wanted." She pointed. "I think what I wanted is being put in the garage."

"Do I even want to know what is going on?" Gavin asked.

She turned to him. "Good morning."

"Good morning, Hannah," he smiled.

She looked at Trevor.

"What did you tell him you wanted?"

"I told him American Muscle, probably from the late sixties. I said it had to compete with a Corvette that had been rebuilt and I said it needed lots of work. I figured we could get the tools as we go. Or not, maybe you want them all now?"

"What is she talking about?"

"She's talking about a checkbook I need to hide. How much?"

"Does it matter? I wasn't worried about the profit margin."

He glared at her.

"Three thousand. Plus five hundred to deliver. Is that bad?"

Trevor looked at Gavin and Gavin looked back.

Gavin shrugged. "That doesn't sound bad depending on what it got us."

Robert came over, she signed the papers, and wrote the check.

A minute later, Trevor and Gavin stared at the wreck. First one laughed. Then the other.

"What?" she asked.

"What did you tell them?"

"Exactly what I said."

Trevor laughed more. "You didn't tell them what?"

She shook her head. "No. Why? Is there a problem?"

"Honey," he said, pointing. "That's a Judge."

They both looked at her.

"What?"

"Pontiac GTO Judge. Out of the cars that could arrive, we will be working on a Judge."

They raided her office—with permission—right after they ate a bowl of cereal. Snagging a digital camera, a blank notebook, some pens and they were ready to work.

"Would a laptop help?" she asked,

They looked between each other.

"Never done that before," Gavin said. "Might be a good way to track sh—"

She smiled. They were cutting off more words these days. She went to the cupboard in the hall, pulled out the bottom drawer and pulled a computer off the stack of computers.

"You built those, didn't you?"

She looked in the drawer before sliding it shut. "Not all of them."

Trevor smiled at her, turned and headed down the hall with Gavin.

She found them a half hour later in the midst of analyzing their treasure. Watching them laugh and smile and play with the knobs and handles, she knew she had given them a jolt of good times.

When she walked in, Gavin shot off some photos of her, making her smile. He came closer, posing with her for a selfie, before he aimed the camera back at Trevor and the Judge.

She set three bottles of cranberry juice on the workbench and watched them move around the wreck. The Hollies sang on the laptop, making her bite her lip and sway.

"Trevor," she said, as he came around to the driver's door to open it and lean in. He looked at her.

"Why did you say you didn't have a traditional relationship with Janice?"

His eyes widened a fraction, the smile guilty. The hood jerked a little with a muted snap. He moved out of the car without answering her and popped the hood.

"Major work in here," he said, looking at it.

Gavin came around with the camera. "Rust is fairly moderate. I think its looks worse than it is. Nothing stood out as totaled."

"Are you going to paint it?" she asked.

"Yes we are," Trevor said, then glanced at her. "Assuming we get the right tools."

"I like yellow."

They looked at her, laughing.

"It's a Judge," Gavin said.

"Okay," she grinned, opening her juice. "That means something?"

"Honey," Trevor said, "Judges are red. *Always* red. And we'll have to find the decals it needs."

She bit her lip again and stared at him. He looked like a man given a booster shot of happy. Both of them did, though she seemed to watch Trevor more.

What she saw now was an energy created by staring at something they truly loved.

He went to the computer, pulled up a search engine and brought up a photo of a restored Judge, turning the computer so she can see. He pointed at the places where decals sat.

"See, to make it right, we have to get all the pieces together, cleaned, painted and perfect."

"Can we get a new license plate?"

He looked at Gavin who shrugged.

"Probably. You would have to do it, but yeah, if that's what you want. What do you want it to say?"

She grabbed the notebook, grabbed a thick Sharpie and leaned over the workbench to write in bold letters.

Smiling, the corner of her lip under her teeth, she held the piece of paper by its horizontal edges and showed it to them.

MYOTLWS.

CHAPTER SIX

Showers to get rid of grease, a dinner of hot dogs and beans, chocolate pudding for dessert. Then billiards instead of TV.

Trevor played with the stereo, finding satellite station, setting it to soft classic rock. He adjusted the volume while Gavin checked the cues by rolling them on the billiard table, making sure they were straight.

Hannah brought in a tray of sliced turkey wraps, spinach wraps, cheese and some grapes.

Recently fed, Gavin took one of the wraps, moaning as he ate. "I swear to God, in our best circumstances, we never ate like you feed us."

"I'm sorry. I can stop if it's a bother in cholesterol or weight or something."

He batted her on her nose with a smile and took more.

She watched Trevor make the break, moving a scattering of colored balls around the table. A solid went in. He moved to line up the next shot. Rum was in the glasses tonight.

They looked more relaxed. More satisfied.

She wondered how wicked it was to think that maybe she helped with that.

"Hannah," Trevor said.

She broke out of her thoughts and looked at him.

"Your shot," he said.

"Oh," she jumped off her stool and moved to the table. She may have grown up with the table, but using it was rare. She sucked and she knew it.

"What are you thinking so hard about?" Trevor asked. "Left us and everything."

She liked his smile, liked his teasing. Saw something there she didn't know was real or imagined.

"Seemed to have succeeded with my last project," she said. "Just trying to think of what to work on next."

She shot the solid; it banked, hit the edge of the pocket then bounced back onto the table. She playfully exaggerated the stomp of her foot and the raspberry she made.

There really wasn't a game of pool for all of them, but the boys shot their game and let her jump in, playing on both sides.

She looked up and Trevor was smiling at her.

"Payday," Gavin said, lining up his shot.

Her gaze came up as he shot. The balls hit and she didn't hear them. Not with that statement sitting on the table with all the stripes and solids.

"What about Payday?" she asked softly. She would swear a ticking clock started in her head.

Trevor took the next shot. "We never found him. Got in the right neighborhood, but there was always too many people around. Too many guards."

"You wanted to?"

He straightened and looked at her.

She stood still, leaning on the stool, the cue in her hands and began to calculate. Only this equation was never going to come together.

"Hannah?" Trevor asked, taking a sip from the glass of rum.

She blew out a hard breath, walking toward the table. She put her stick on the green felt, and then stared at it as she held on to the bumper.

"Payday Morgan," she said, "Everything comes back to Payday."

"He was an influential person in our lives," Gavin said. "He was responsible for what happened."

"I know," she said.

"Hannah," Trevor asked. "What? You look like you've seen a ghost. What aren't you saying?"

She stared at the table and held on tight. "Payday Morgan died April 18th, two years ago." She brought her gaze up.

They stared at her.

"*Whaaat?*" Trevor choked.

"He went to South America."

"We heard that. Even inside we heard that. What the fuck do you know?"

"He died."

They stared at her.

Gavin stepped forward. "This guy was responsible for destroying every aspect of our lives. If you have information about him, say something."

She walked to a stool and sat on the edge. They followed to stand in front of her.

"You have to understand," she said, "I didn't tell you because I didn't not want you to know. I didn't tell because I didn't want you to know how it happened and why. If I told you he was dead, you were going to ask questions."

"Humor us," Trevor said. He walked to put his stick on the table by hers then moved to fill their glasses with more rum.

"That week in April, Payday was called to Columbia. His boss, Javier Escobar wanted a face to face. Payday never came back."

"Okay, he never came back. Why did he never come back?"

"I met him," she said, bringing her gaze to Trevor's.

"What?" he gasped.

"Before I was invested—before I knew I was going to do this with you, I was checking out all resources. I needed to know so I could decide. I called and said I was a reporter. He wanted the interview and I met with him at this restaurant. Very posh. It was called Maple Bristo."

"That is nice," Trevor said.

"He had the back room and it was only him and I and I knew his people were everywhere and how risky it was, but I needed the info."

"There is no information in the world worth that. This motherfucker killed people. Did he hurt you?"

"He tried at the end. Before I left."

"Payday decides you're going to be his next lay, and you walked out?"

"Yes. He never touched me."

"You were strapped with explosives?" Gavin asked.

"Better. I had his social and the last four on three of his credit cards. That freaked him and he threw me out. Literally. I was dragged to a back door and thrown out. I found a taxi. I was pretty shaken up."

"You got away from Payday Morgan, who thinks rape and murder are fun afternoon social activities?"

"He was drunk and coked-up when I got there. He kept going with both, talking non-stop. He went for five hours so I sat there and memorized it all."

"You can do that?"

She nodded.

Gavin closed his eyes and sank onto a chair. Trevor stayed standing, staring. His gaze wasn't accusatory, though.

"Do you want to hear this? It's really bad and it directly affects you."

"I'm supposed to say no to that?"

She waited, took a drink. "I'm sorry I didn't tell you." She smiled tight and looked at him.

He waited.

"After the...at your place, the shooters went to Payday. They told him everything. From the moment they walked in the door, until they left."

"Hannah, we know what happened. We know what they did. You have to tell us what he said."

"No you don't," she said. "You don't know they did it on purpose."

"What?" his voice dropped.

"They knew they were in the wrong house, right away. They decided to continue."

"Why?"

She brought her gaze to his. "I was told it was fun."

Gavin gasped. Trevor lost his voice.

"And Lucas, he was—" she stopped and looked at him.

"What about Lucas?"

She looked at him. "I know how he died."

"You know more about my brother's death than I do?"

"I think so. And I don't think you need to hear the details I have."

"Does it have to do with Payday?"

"Yes, but no. But yes."

"You're sure about that?"

She smiled a little.

"Hannah, please."

"Lucas died last," she said, bringing her gaze up. "Ceaser wanted to leave. Too much death, I guess. He didn't want to kill Lucas. But Lucas wouldn't stop crying Payday told me. Jojo didn't like babies. He hated the noise so he…the powder burns on him, on Lucas, they were flush and in the shape of a barrel." she let her voice trail away.

Trevor closed his eyes, lowered his chin and rubbed the back of his neck. "Lucas was fussy," he said, looking at her with damp eyes. "He always was. There had to be blo…he had to know Mom was…"

His gaze dropped again.

"Payday told me he liked it."

Trevor's gaze snapped up. "He liked what?"

"Payday liked that Jojo would do that for him. He said it was the ultimate in loyalty. He wanted to see more. He thought his people, if they could be called that, would prove they would do anything for him."

She paused, taking a breath, looking at the ground.

"What?"

She brought her gaze up. "Four days after I met Payday, a kid named Diego Bishop, sixteen years old, was caught breaking into a house. The dad got up and found Diego outside his daughter's room. He was a Payday recruit, he was armed with a full clip and suppressor. The baby was eight months. Her name was Cicely."

"You're fucking kidding me?"

"It was Payday. I knew it. I looked in his computer and there was all sorts of stuff like this in there."

Trevor turned to look at her. "How do you know the date?"

"How?" Gavin snapped, switching directions. "How did he die? Gunshot like ours, sword fight, fucking shark attack?"

Her eyes closed and her chin lowered.

"Shark attack?" Gavin said in disbelief, getting out of his seat, still holding his cue. "You're going to say it was a fucking shark attack?"

She looked at him. "He died horribly and it took a while and it was more painful than you can imagine."

"Not painful enough," Trevor said.

Her gaze dropped. "His boss," she said, soft. "Javier Escobar. He demanded this meeting and while Payday was there, Escobar took Payday deep sea fishing. They left port on the 18th. When the boat came in late that afternoon, they had a ton of fish and no Payday."

"Escobar tossed him in?"

She stared at the floor, her gut hurting. "I have money, brains and I can use a computer to find what you want hidden." She looked up at Trevor. "Escobar had an unhappy bodyguard. He was there. He gave me every detail which is typed up and pretty. It's on my desktop of my computer. I read it about once a week. The bodyguard gave it to me and then disappeared with my two million dollars."

She walked over to sink onto a bar stool and tried to hide.

"You spent two million dollars to get this?" Gavin asked.

She didn't answer.

"Why didn't you tell us?"

"I didn't want you to know how it happened."

"How did it happen?"

She stared at the floor. "Escobar got hold of information suggesting Payday was cheating him. That's why he called for the meeting."

"Oh fuck, Hannah. What did you do?" Trevor asked softly.

"I broke into Payday's computer. And his attorney's computer. And his accountant's computer." She shrugged. "I sent everything to Columbia."

"And that's what you didn't want us to know. Shit. You know you're not really related to us and shouldn't take on this shit for us."

"I'm sorry," she said. She couldn't look at either of them. "Payday was shot twice in the shoulder and thrown overboard screaming. And yes, shark attacks are rare around there, but from what I understand this was one of those times. If you want to read the file, I have it. I was going to give it to you. Sometime. I think. I just didn't know when."

She got up, turned and headed out the door.

Trevor stood by the billiard table, his arms wide set, his head bowed with closed eyes. He couldn't even put a definition on the concept that it really might all be over with the death of Payday. That she had hid that? He didn't put anything to that other than she really was afraid of what they would think of her when they found out.

He could throw her further than he could blame her.

He pushed off the table, standing straight. Gavin's face, pale. His body looked limp.

"Do you want to read that file?" Trevor asked in a breathless voice.

"No," Gavin said, without hesitation.

And he didn't have to explain why, not to Trevor. Gavin was the softer of the two. He would walk away from the history faster. Though he would never forgive anyone for what they took, he wouldn't stand still and live with pain. He had too big a heart and too strong a will.

He would never blame a beautiful woman for wanting to care.

Neither would Trevor.

"Can you excuse me?" he asked Gavin formerly.

He followed her, finding her in her chair, staring at the screen with all the lights off in the room.

"Can I come in?" he asked from the door. His hands were in his pockets.

She didn't answer so he came in anyway.

He got all the way to her desk, his thighs leaning up against the wood in the front.

"I left that deposit bag by the front door, in the drawer," she said without looking at him. "Money, ID. Everything you need. I can take care of monitoring from here. You'll be safe."

"I need you to listen and to really pay attention, okay?"

She looked at him and he hated the sorrow on her soft features. He saw a person who thought she already lost what she wanted to keep.

"This is kinda hard to appreciate. But Mom and Aunt Lucy, they were not like other Moms. They knew what they wanted and their men left and then it was them teaching us what we needed to know. They drilled into all of us you always keep moving forward, no matter what shit life hands you. Gavin and me, we learned real young that we wouldn't be allowed to ever live with regrets."

"What does that mean?" she asked, soft.

"It means we did what we did and when we were done the rage was gone, but we didn't solve anything. Everyone was still dead and not coming back and we still hurt from it, and we live with that while trying to have a life. Now, because of you, we are together and we don't wear orange. We had to come to terms, both of us, with acknowledging what we lost so we could move forward."

"I don't understand."

"You didn't need to tell us not to go to the cemetery. We knew the last time we were there would be the last time we were there. And you were right, we did decide to do it there after two bottles of Jacks, sitting on the graves. The night guard used to let us stay there in sleeping bags on the grass. I seriously do not want to tell you how often we did it."

"I never read that."

"We never told anyone. Neither did the guard."

He came forward, around the desk, leaning onto the wood. He slipped the mouse from her hand and clicked on her desk top.

There in the bottom right hand corner was a Payday Candy Bar icon. It had to be one she made herself since it was so much larger than the others. It was a constant reminder of what she thought she did. She didn't need to be reading it once a week.

"Do you have any hard copies?" he asked.

"No."

He put the cursor over the icon, right clicked and it disappeared.

Payday disappeared.

"You know I can find that."

He put his hand on hers. "No, Hannah. You can't. It's gone. It doesn't exist anymore. Okay? For us? Let it go?"

"I killed him. That doesn't change the good girl image?"

"I always leaned more toward Wonder Woman, remember?"

She smiled a little, even as a tear slipped down her cheek.

"Did you add anything to that document you sent?"

"No. It was only what I pulled off their computers."

"So you took a corrupt and evil man, gave his secrets to a corrupt and evil man and stood back to see what happened. They did it to themselves, Hannah. You need to understand that right this minute. You didn't pull any triggers."

He stood close, right at her side, his arm brushing hers.

Using his body, he pushed on her chair so it turned more toward him.

Leaning close, he put his palm to her cheek, brushing away the damp with his thumb. He stared at her, seeing strength in the virtue.

Women he had known, usually they had finished high school, and that was good. Even in the jobs at a salon or a department store, there was an element in them he liked. Looking at Hannah, he stared at what was in front of him. She didn't stand in the wealth and education that others might use to define themselves. She was a woman who turned toward what she saw as a wrong and helped the people she never should have cared about. Whether it was them or one of the silent victims she found justice for.

He was caught, he thought with a small smile and he might as well admit it.

His hand shifted to the tip of her chin, pulling her face toward his as he leaned in close, his lips resting on hers with an electoral jolt. Her lip balm was strawberry flavored. He hadn't known that and he liked finding out like this. He glided his mouth only a little.

She kissed him back, her soft hands on his forearms, her warm lips moving enough to make him think wild.

Gavin cleared his throat in the doorway. Trevor pulled back to what could almost be considered civil distance from her, keeping her stare.

"What?" he asked Gavin, watching her blush.

"I made microwave popcorn since we needed it faster than regular. There were four Hershey Bars left and I put the Cokes in the TV Room."

"You going somewhere with this?" Trevor asked Gavin, while still staring at her.

"I got *The Odd Couple* fired up. The original. I think when Felix clears his sinuses; I thought we could use that right now."

"What do you think," Trevor asked her, stepping back to a respectable distance.

She stared at his mouth, taking a slow, deep breath. That might be the biggest turn on yet.

"I like *The Odd Couple,*" she said. "Did you know Jack Lemmon and Walter Matthau are buried almost next to each other?"

"I did not know that," he smiled. He held out his hand. She stared at it for a second then bit her lip. She reached up and took the offer.

CHAPTER SEVEN

The night's revelations were not allowed to poison the house.

"He took too much," Trevor said over the breakfast of pancakes and sausage. "I'm not giving him anymore."

She ate in silence. He watched her work it out. Gavin leaned over, wrapped his arm around her and pulled her close to put his forehead on hers.

"We took a vote while you were in the shower," he said.

She leaned away while he held on, blinking at him. Trevor picked up his last piece of sausage and ate it bit by bit.

"We decided you way outrank us in purity of motives, so in order to stick around, we have to grovel to you and put you on this pedestal that's been waiting."

She stared down but smiled. He pulled her close, kissed her on the forehead, then looked to Trevor, raising his eyebrows before clearing his plate.

"What are you going to do today?" Trevor asked.

"Missing husband and father of one. She's an adult. The daughter is requesting the case be reopened to locate her dad so she can bust her mom."

"Sweet," he said. "Family reunions. Will you be long? There was a discussion I was hoping to continue with you."

She looked at him, blushed, and then cleared her plate.

She leaned back on the counter, to look at him. He turned in his chair for a better view.

"Should be an almost easy case. I have a general location and the times I need. Then I was planning on taking some time off later this afternoon to..." she smiled, shy. "See what is going on."

"Maybe you should get to work then, work fast. We'll see what happens."

She got her coffee then disappeared down the hall.

He cleaned up, met Gavin in the garage and moved forward on disassembly so they could work on the rust. The music was good, the company better and he had hopes of furthering relationships he hadn't anticipated.

Coming into the kitchen he saw her heading out the backdoor, turning to walk to the rear of the property.

He followed her, keeping his distance. She entered a small shed off the gravel path and pulled the door shut behind her.

Standing at the door, he leaned in, putting his ear to the wood. No sound came.

He pushed the handle and saw her standing next to a work bench. She looked over her shoulder at him and smiled.

"Thought you were working," she said.

He pursed his lips and shook his head, coming further into the small room. It was garden shed, with pots and shovels and piles of packaged soil.

"Gavin's checking the undercarriage for rust."

"I think you can assume on that one."

"We're probably going to start a list of things we need. We'll call it a loan and square up later."

"Yeah," she smiled. "I was worried about that."

"What are you doing?"

He moved closer, aware of the shape of her, the look of her. From the back, he saw her in jeans and appreciated it. He moved closer.

"I was going to start dinner pretty soon, but my pan broke."

"What's wrong with it?"

"The handle is loose," she said.

He was close enough behind her to realize the sense of trust it took for her to put her back to him. She wasn't afraid of him. She really never had been.

"What's for dinner?"

"A frittata."

"A what?"

"Eggs, potato, cheese. It has to bake in the oven, though, so it has to be this pan. The handle can take the temperature."

When he stepped close enough to put his chin on her shoulder, she sucked in a startled breath and froze, screwdriver in one hand, the pan in another.

"That sounds real good," he whispered, leaning his chest to her back, his hands coming around her to rest on the workbench in front of her.

Her face turned toward him. "What are you doing?"

"I was going to help you fix your pan. I want to eat and I like when you cook. Maybe this one will be the best."

"Can you help me from over there?" she pointed to the side.

He ran his hands down her arms until he held the backs of hers under his.

He spoke softly in her ear. "Flatten out your palms."

He felt her tremble against him, her whole body shaking when a minute ago it had been steady. She hesitated only a few seconds before sliding her fingers out, her palms to the smooth wood, her fingers spreading wide.

Pretty, natural nails. No rings.

He marveled again at a bank account he knew could afford more. The scent was so similar to the shampoo in his bathroom. It mingled with her own chemistry and created something he liked. Her hair tickled his nose as he snuggled closer into the nook.

"Your hands can't move off that table," he said, soft. "Do you know that?"

"I think I'm figuring it out."

Slowly, he moved his hands on her arms and then he put them on her waist. With summer lingering, it was still hot. She wore a white tank top over the jeans. His fingers dipped in from the edge of the shirt and down into the edge of her jeans.

He kissed her on the space beside her ear. "You say stop. I will stop."

His hands didn't move as he waited, praying for the right answer.

"Don't stop," she said, almost too soft to be heard. His own pulse picked up and his breathing took a turn towards fast. She leaned back onto him, the back of her head on his shoulder.

Very slowly using both hands, he unfastened the button on her jeans, pulling the zipper low enough to make room for his fingers, flat against her skin. The other hand traveled north while she purred. It moved up, under her tank, edging into the line of the bra until he felt the crease of her breast.

He didn't push further, but nuzzled her neck, his eyes closed tight. It had been too many years since he had a woman in his arms. Being luckily enough to find his perfect fit on the first time, there were no words.

"Is this fair to Gavin?" she whispered.

"Do you have a cousin?" he asked.

She put a hand on his forearms, the skin exposed, touching him like a lover before they had taken that step.

"We have dinner soon. Then probably a movie," she said.

"Would be expected." He kissed her hard on the neck, sucking lightly.

Her voice was soft. "I could leave my door unlocked tonight at bedtime. I mean, if you want."

Her voice trembled, her body stiff.

He pulled both his hands off her, put them on her shoulder and spun her to face him.

Her shy grin looked sexy. He held onto her shoulders tight.

"What do you mean by that?"

The mood shattered in the heartbeat, he stared at her.

"Excuse me?" she blinked. Her breath changed, still hard but with a different rhythm. Her eyes only a little wide.

"What you just said." His anger came on fast, not making sense even to him. She couldn't have meant what she said.

"Um," her expression changing. Bright eyes turned dull from turned-on to confused. He felt her trying to lean away but she was trapped against the bench.

Her gaze dropped. The look changed from sexy to scared. "I thought I was issuing an invitation but if I misread this situation, I'm sorry."

Feeling the constant reminder of what he had been, it didn't fit she would have said it. But she had. And he didn't like being pulled side to side.

"I didn't mean disrespect," she said soft.

"Disrespect?" he snapped, then laughed. "That's the kind of thing you say in the yard to the guy who's got fifty pounds on you and wants to rip your arms off."

He scared her with that one. He saw it and felt guilty.

"What you said," he said.

"I don't know what I said. I don't know what I did. I thought we were getting along."

"You'll unlock your door," he pointed out.

"Yes, I said that."

"The only way you can unlock your door, is if you've been keeping it locked all along."

She looked down, her eyes darting side to side. She shook under his touch.

Her gaze snapped up. "No," she said, husky with a little laugh. "That's not what I meant."

"You're not keeping your door locked since you got company?"

"I always keep my door locked. I always have. Even when I'm home alone. I was raised in boarding school. When I got my own room, I learned to keep it locked."

"So if it's not the convict, why all the stress right now?" he asked.

"I never called you that. I just don't do well with rejection. I have a feeling that's what is happening and I need to go. I can't do this. I do this too much."

He stared without saying anything. Pulling in his own misplaced reaction to the fear he saw now, there were a few things they still needed to discuss.

"Please let me go."

She was afraid of him when she never had been before. He dropped his hands. She fixed her clothes and picked up her pan, heading toward the door, turning before she got there. There was a certain level of hell for him when he saw her eyes damp from this brief exchange. Something had happened and he had started it.

"Your story is one of the most horrific I have ever heard," she said. "I think of what they took and I cry for you but I can't help but know that for a while you had a family who loved you and you loved them. Some of us never got that. Some us were kicked out of our families when they were nine years old. We didn't get what you had so please excuse me when I say bugger off, forget the offer and stay away from me."

She disappeared fast, the door banging shut. He had his first clue of what she might be hiding.

While she went to the kitchen to put on dinner, he went to the garage and ignored Gavin's request to help with rust. Going to the house to wander the halls, looking a lot deeper than he had before. He went so far as to snoop in her bedroom. The sorrow hid there, too. Very little signaled a real person lived here.

Her expensive three tiered jewelry box was empty. No earrings, no treasures, no secret mementos from school.

There were no riches on her night stand. Not a favorite childhood book, an old diary or an autograph book from when she was ten. There wasn't a photo of a life that might have existed before she became who she was.

He went to the garage where the Judge was starting to look like a project. Pieces were being pulled and cleaned in the tank she had arranged for.

Gavin was busy with a fender. He had the rock-n-roll playing as always—Guns-n-Roses—while Trevor stared at the spiral staircase that rose in the corner.

He had been upstairs once with Gavin, just to look around when they had run out of nooks and crannies to explore. He hadn't done more than peeking under the cloth over the paintings.

Hannah had loved her Grandmother dearly, that was obvious by the way the entire studio and office had been preserved.

"When you spoke to her," Trevor asked, "did she mention any family, any friends?"

"No family besides her grandparents, but she said she still kept a few friends in the city. She said she didn't see them or talk to them much."

"So she hangs out in 10,000 square feet with a cat."

"I got the feeling she was more comfortable with that."

"What about a boyfriend? Or even a girlfriend? Any relationships?"

"I asked. I got the feeling she was straight, but she didn't say enough to put a story behind any of it. Why?"

Trevor stood and looked at him. "Why don't you hang out around here? I need to figure something out."

"Do I want to know?"

"Not right now."

"If you hurt her, you and I will have a serious disagreement."

The threat was real.

"If I do, I will let you win."

Trevor blew out a sharp breath and turned toward those stairs.

Big windows captured the light in the elongated room. There were drips of colored paint on the floor—reds, blues, purples. The fact the last painting Maureen had been working on, a painting of bright colors and beautiful skies, only partially done, reminded him he had crossed too many lines.

Maureen died six years ago, yet the smell of turpentine and oils still permeated the room. On the opposite side was a sectioned off portion.

He stared at the long ago used desk, where the only photo he had seen of Hannah laughing with her grandmother sat. Hannah had Maureen's eyes. He smiled and picked it, stared, thought about stealing it, and then set it back down.

Moving to sit in the desk chair, he started in the drawers, going through each one carefully. He didn't know what he wanted but he knew it was here. When he finished with the drawers, he moved to the file cabinets.

In forty-five minutes, sweaty from the heat of the loft, he had the file he suspected: the letter exchange between Gr'ma Maureen and Hannah's very likely insane mother.

I don't do rejection well. I've had too much.

He leaned back in the chair, closed his eyes and slammed the pile of papers against his thigh. "You fucking bitch," he said to the room. "She was your daughter."

In a miscommunication during the sexiest exchange of his life, he had driven her away with no force. She had run as fast as she could as if she had been running her whole God damn life.

CHAPTER SEVEN

"That was great," Gavin grinned as he pushed the plate away.

She smiled, feeling some satisfaction that she could still do this.

"I love a little hostility to go with my meal."

Her smile fell with the intake of a breath at the comment, staring at her plate, ignoring Trevor across the table with his glass of wine. Hiding emotions was something she knew about.

"I'm sorry," she said, trying to smile. "I had some things come up today that were distracting. I shouldn't have let them come to dinner."

She looked at Gavin but he wasn't paying attention to her. He stared at his plate.

"Let me ask a question," Trevor asked, saying his first words since the meal started.

She forced herself to look at him. "What?"

"What the hell were you doing in a boarding school when you were nine years old?"

Gavin's gaze snapped to hers. "You were where?"

The question caught her totally off guard though she knew she had set it up. Delving into her past was never on her agenda and she wasn't starting now.

"My family," she said. "They were located in a more rural area. For a good education I had to go away to school."

Trevor nodded and took a sip of his wine. "That explains it. So tell me why your family sent you to boarding school when you were nine-years-old?"

"What are you doing?" Gavin asked. "Let it go."

"I get an honest answer, I'll let it go."

"I answered you," she said, taking a stand against the blue eyes.

He leaned forward on the table. "You think you know everything there is to know about us? I want to know one fact about you. Why weren't you home with your family?"

"All I know about you is what I needed to accomplish this so you could have decent dinner you didn't have to stand in line for."

"Trevor," Gavin snapped. "Shut the fuck up."

Hannah's gaze jumped to him but she didn't correct the swear.

"Why did your family put you in a kiddy prison?"

"It was a school. A good one. I got a fantastic education."

"You don't know everything," Trevor said.

"I never said I did," she kept the challenge.

"Dayo Conde." He said the words slowly.

Gavin's gaze snapped to Trevor's while she stared with no air in her lungs.

"I happen to know the order and who did who, when, how we set it up and how long it took to pull off. Six different men all with the same results."

"What. The fuck. Are you doing?" Gavin snapped.

"Shut up," Trevor said. "Why did your folks send you to boarding school when you were nine?"

"It doesn't matter and it's none of your business and I do not want to know any more about you."

"He loved his car," Trevor said. "Bastard loved that fucking car. He kept it in the garage in the basement away from all the other cars. He was our first but Gavin wasn't ready so I went down while Gavin stood guard. I hid behind the pillar next to the parking space. When Conde came in he had some friends and I thought for sure I was dead. He was going to find me, know who I was and that was it. But he didn't. They left and he didn't even get the car started before he died in its front seat."

Knowing her color faded, she stared at the table while her palms sweated.

"That was one. Answer my question."

"I answered you."

"JoJo Gallo—"

She snapped her gaze up. "Every name you give up, you are revealing his list and that isn't fair."

"No, it actually isn't," Gavin grinned sarcastically.

"JoJo was with his girlfriend so I had to wait. We never went after anyone—"

"My mother," she snapped, her gaze locking on his. "My mother wanted me gone so my father said yes and I was gone. I played chess with my mother and she didn't want me anymore. Do you have any other questions or should I get dessert? I made chocolate cake."

Trevor leaned back in his seat, sighed hard and stared at her.

"That's the honest answer."

She stood up without clearing anything and left with her wine glass.

Gavin glared at Trevor. "You have a reason for divulging that one thing we promised we would never divulge?"

Trevor stared at the last inch of his wine. "Wasn't worth keeping if I could use it to help her. I'm sorry. I should have asked you first."

He shifted his gaze to meet Gavin's. Trevor knew he had violated two trusts.

"This is what you were talking about before?"

Trevor stood from the table and went after her. Only she wasn't in the kitchen and the house was too big to make a search easy.

She was on a back porch off the second floor on the other side of the building, overlooking the backyard. She stood at the railing; her arms crossed a glass in hand, a new bottle on the railing.

He didn't say anything in the dark, not even when Gavin found them a minute later. He stood and watched and waited.

She didn't turn around.

"My mother was a chess master. Not something well known. It didn't sit well with her society friends. But she was good. Damn good."

Neither man broke the silence.

"When I was nine years old, I asked her to play with me. She didn't like me all that much and I knew it. She wasn't exactly subtle. I guess I was thinking if we did this, maybe she would want to spend more time with me."

She turned to face him and he hadn't been expecting the thick tears.

"I'm smart," she said.

"We kinda figured that out."

"No," she said. "You think you have, but what you have seen is very little because I hide. I hide because people get weird when they know. That night with my mother, I beat her at chess in four moves."

"Impressive," Gavin said.

"So what, you're like Einstein?" Trevor asked.

She looked away. "Einstein's IQ, is thought to be in the 160 range. I would kill to be that stupid."

Trevor thought about that. He didn't know a lot about IQ's but he thought for her it might be an important measuring stick people forced on her.

"She went nuts," Hannah said. "She said I was a freak. She told my father she didn't want me in the house and he didn't said no to her. She needed help. Professional help but he never wanted to admit there was a problem. Two days later I was living in The Ashville Institute. I had one suitcase, the clothes on my back and a dorm I shared with three other girls."

She leaned a little forward. "I was nine years old."

"Your Mom had trouble with kids?" Gavin asked.

"Not really. She did fine with my brother and sister."

"You have a brother and a sister?" Trevor asked.

"One older, one younger. From what I understand they are all still happy together. They visited me four times, came for graduation and then I never saw any of them again. I spent my free time here with my grandparents."

Trevor took a step toward her. "Do you understand the concept of no secrets? In what you do, in what you did for us?"

"I never lied," she said. "I didn't tell you about me, but that's not lying."

He looked at her. "Hannah," he said. He put a hand on his chest. "JoJo Gallo, Dayo Conde and Steve Bundy."

Gavin drew a hard breath and let it out. "Ceaser De La Cruz, Mike Morales and David Silva."

Trevor could see her shaking.

"Why?" she whispered. "You never admitted that to anyone, not even for lesser sentences."

"Because I don't want secrets between us. I don't think he does either. You can tell me anything and it will be okay."

"How did you figure that?"

Trevor looked over at Gavin who paused, nodded his head then left the way he came, giving them privacy.

"I made a mistake in our exchange earlier. I thought you were calling me a criminal and I didn't like it."

"I would never do that."

"Which is what I knew so there had to be a reason. In those few seconds something sparked in you that looked like fear, but you're not afraid of me. Or you weren't until I blew it. So I looked. And I went too far. I found your mother's letters in your grandmother's studio."

"You read Gr'ma's letters?"

"No, I read you mothers. And only a couple. Only enough to confirm what I suspected."

He saw the fragile woman he hadn't seen before. She had been hurt to inhuman proportions by people who should have loved her for her astronomical abilities and compassionate and generous nature.

"She raised you," he said.

She looked away. "Gr'ma M kept me in that school but I was here the rest of the time. Mom and Dad hid sending me there from her a long time. Then Gr'ma showed up and let me know they wouldn't bother me anymore. She never spoke to them again, either. My mother was their only child."

She looked at him.

"She put me in every educational program she could find. Gr'ma and Gr'pa never gave up on me."

"I'm sorry I scared you. I wouldn't do that on purpose. I hope you know that."

"You don't think I'm a freak?" she asked, soft.

He smiled. "When you say chocolate cake, do you mean like a standard chocolate cake or did you do something gourmet and fancy?"

She watched the wood planks of the porch. "Two layers. Chocolate frosting."

"Ice cream?" he grinned.

She nodded.

"I think that sounds really good."

Her chin came up, her gaze on his. "You don't have to pretend."

"What am I pretending?"

"There's milk, too. For the cake. I might have to run to the market tomorrow, though."

He moved closer to her. "What am I pretending?"

"Please. Don't," she whispered. He could hear the tears in her voice. "Just let it go."

Another step toward her. He was close enough to see her strong resolve was making her shake.

"What am I pretending?"

She looked at him. "I'm not good at relationships."

"I wasn't asking for a relationship. I was discussing my views on chocolate cake. I'm sorta curious what you think."

"I think the cake is in the kitchen."

He took that final step, bringing her next to him. He stood there, letting her feel him, letting her get used to something he had the feeling she wasn't used to.

A man who cared.

Her shaking was visible, her fear pronounced. He could feel her heavy breaths, but she didn't look at him. She stared at his chest.

"Is your offer still open?" he asked quietly.

She looked up then, surprised.

"The lock on your door?"

Her gaze dropped again and instead of heavy breathing, she stopped all together.

He leaned forward to whisper in her ear.

"I would like to sleep with you tonight and when I say that, I do mean sleep. I want to see you in the morning when you first open your eyes."

Her gaze snapped and he saw her pull in strength.

"Is this the line you use to get women into bed?"

"Been quite a while since I tried to get a woman into bed but no, I don't think this was ever a route of mine. In fact, I can't remember a single woman I ever spent the night with where I realized I wanted to wake up with her more than I wanted to stay awake with her."

After ice cream and cake, they insisted they watch *The Princess Bride*, after finding out it was her favorite. They said goodnight and each went to their own rooms.

Letting out a hard breath, Hannah stood in her pristine bedroom suite. Messing her hair to look stylishly sexy, she changed her day make-up to soft with a hint of smoke. Then she stripped down, the spit bath didn't take long. Lotion and powder was applied with a loving touch to achieve the full effect.

Seducing a man was actually something she did know a little about.

Seducing one who made her heart race while turning everything she felt into a smile? She hadn't done that before. And now, when she had been fairly sure of where they were heading, this afternoon had left her shaken enough for history to seep into something she had really wanted.

She wasn't very good with men. Relationships always ended badly. But she liked him. A lot. For a little while, maybe he would like her.

The plunging neckline and bare thighs from the black satin kimono brought her confidence. Moving slow, she lit the lavender purple scented candle by the bed, pulled out several condom packs and put them by the candle then turned off the light. Walking across the room, she unlocked the door.

Sitting on the edge of the bed, her feet on the running board, she waited in the dark alphabetizing all the countries in the world in her head. She started with Afghanistan and worked her way up to Guinea-Bissau knowing she wasn't missing any or out of order. She was all the way to Paraguay when the door knob jerked, paused, then turned. Her breath hung in her chest, her hands trembling as he closed the door, flicked the lock and moved toward her in the shadows.

She tried to lift her gaze, but it was frozen about his belly-button level.

He stood directly in front of her, close enough to touch. Grey sweatpants, a NCIS long sleeve T-shirt, his feet bare. He took a long time to look her over, his breath deepening. He raised a finger to her neck, drawing it down slowly until he hooked into the satin of the robe.

"I think we might have had a misunderstanding." His finger slid under the edge, pushing the material to the side, heading toward her shoulder. He took time to appreciate the view he exposed.

"I thought you might have changed your mind," she whispered.

Nervously she looked up at him and smiled. His face was different tonight, darker with an edge she had suspected would be there.

"Probably not," he whispered, the back of his knuckle trailing along her chest, the rise of her breast. "But don't take that the wrong way."

Only she did.

Rejection was devastating. Rejection from him—she couldn't even think of what it would be like.

Reaching up, she pulled the edges of her robe a little closer. "I'm sorry," she smiled, "I thought—never mind." Her gaze dropped, hurt burning low in her gut.

"Was this always the plan?"

She looked up at him. "What?"

"Get us out, get us here, get one of us to fall in love with you?"

She froze and pulled away.

His finger went under her chin, pulling her face to look at him. "I was kidding," he said. "I'm pretty happy with our situation."

"Don't, please," she said.

"What?"

"Say things. It's not necessary."

"I don't care if it's necessary or not. I wouldn't say it if they weren't true."

She backed up a little more on the bed. "You don't have to say that to me. It's not necessary. I can be whatever you want. Just no promises."

He leaned closer, his eyes closing.

She jumped back when his mouth got close to hers.

He paused, opening his eyes to stare at her.

She couldn't look at him. "You're not supposed to care. It's supposed to be easy and you don't care."

He waited a few breaths then backed up a bit, his hands dropping away. "Hannah," he said. "I'm not here because it's convenient or because it's been awhile. I'm here because of you…you for a long time with me."

She reached up and held him by the hand.

It was hard to breath, but so much rode on her words.

"Michael and I went to a play on a Monday."

"The play was called *Disturbed Chocolate*. It was a comedy. It was good. I had fun. Afterwards we met Jill and Mark for a late dinner and then we went home."

She took a breath.

"The next day, Tuesday, it was normal. Nothing spectacular from either of us. We both worked late, he brought home Chinese and we ended up watching *Seinfeld* reruns. We had some wine and fooled around on the couch."

She closed her eyes.

"The next day I was getting out of the shower and he was waiting with a big, fluffy towel. He wrapped me in it then turned me to face him. Then he told me he hated me," she said in a monotone. "He said my touch repulsed him. That he had to get drunk to show up for sex. He left me standing there and told me he wanted me gone by the time he got home."

She opened her eyes and he was watching her.

"A couple of years before it was the same with Ken. We were together almost two years and he said pretty much the same things. He wanted me out, too. I always thought that was kinda funny with the two of them."

"Why is that funny?"

"It was my apartment. I owned it free and clear. They both hired help to separate me from it. Michael tried to get a lawyer to figure how to prove I had agreed to this pre-nup when there was no pre-nup. He tried to take half of what I have. That was dumb."

She looked at him. "Men don't like me. Not really. It's the brain and money. I'm fun for a while but not long. They start thinking about it, adding it all up. And I really like you. A lot. And I don't think—"

"What?" he whispered.

"Your Aunt Kira showed me some photos. You were in a chair in a Santa hat with Lucas on your lap and Sarah and Caleb sitting around you. You were reading *A Night Before Christmas*. There was another picture when you were younger. Like maybe a prom. You were with a girl. The photo was candid and she was pretty. You wore a suit with a tie. I never knew her name. You were looking at her in a way that I had always wanted someone to look at me."

"Rachael," he said. "Her name was Rachael and she was a life time ago."

She grinned halfway. "I was sorta sunk after that. I knew I cared about both of you, but one took forefront. I never thought you would want to…not with me."

"You fell in love with an illusion," he said.

She nodded. "At first. I didn't think it would be a problem but then you were here and it got worse and you were nice to me. As long as I could keep most of me from you, you were nice to me."

He knelt in front of her, holding her hands. "Honey, love doesn't get worse. Love makes things better."

She wiped at the tears. "I liked them. Michael, Ken, the rest. I did. We had fun but it was never earth shattering, never a love story. I didn't even miss them all that much when they left."

She looked down. "But if at the end of this time together, when you go, if I have to stand back and have you say those things to me, I don't think I would be able to do very well after that. And that's not fair of me to put that kind of pressure on you so if you want to do this while you're here, I'm okay with that. I just can't handle promises."

He shifted, his arm around her, pulling her close even as he leaned over. He touched her in ways that made her want more. The kiss wasn't like last night. He took her high fast, his hands on her body, his warm tongue gliding on hers.

He pulled back, holding her face, staying close.

She looked down, looking embarrassed. "When people find out you have that kind of money, they generally like you for that kind of money. You never know if it's you they really want or the fact you can pay for the trip to Barbados."

"But you know I don't want your money."

She closed her eyes, smiled. "My whole life I hated having it and I hated being smart. One was bad. Both ..." she laughed a little and opened her eyes. "I was able to do this, to help you both, because I was smart and I had money."

He reached up to run a finger on her cheek. "You know what I can't do?"

She shook her head.

"When I eat out, I can never figure out the tip. It's like my brain goes numb and I have to use fingers to count."

She smiled. "I can do tips."

"What did Michael do for a living?" he asked her with a hand on her shoulder, pushing gently until she fell back on her elbows.

She blinked hard. "He was a photo journalist."

"Ken?" Trevor moved closer, traveling the journey with her from upright to lying down.

"Politics."

"So that's your problem. Now we fixed it. You'll be fine."

She was on her back, and he slid her up on the mattress. The satin slipped to the sides, showing her off. His gaze traveled the length of her before returning to her eyes. He moved to settle his whole body over hers, his thighs between hers, pressing her into the quilt as she squirmed.

She untucked his blue T-shirt from his jeans, pushing her hands under the material to find skin while he kissed along her jaw, her head back, his hands moving in a soft caress on her skin.

He shrugged out of the shirt, throwing it to the floor.

He kissed her throat. "You've been hanging out with highly educated journalist people who think too much. Now you have a criminal who is going to ask himself every day of his life why this gorgeous, educated, generous person ever looked twice at him."

His kiss came harder, deeper, her back arching as he pressed his hips forward, teasing her.

"You gave me more than a chance, Hannah," he whispered. "You gave me a reason."

Still held tight against him, both on their sides facing each other, their legs tangled as she watched his breathing come back to normal, his eyes closed. His skin was damp, the scent that said him—close to her, protecting her.

She reached up to trace the Corvette symbol on his chest. His eyes opened, his grin sincere. He pulled her an inch closer.

"The reason," he said in a breathless voice, "I never considered Janice a traditional relationship is because I never slept with her."

She tilted her chin, confused and thought about that. "That's—why?"

"I never wanted to." He blinked, "I mean, she was willing and offered and there was nothing wrong with either of us. I was with her three or four months. I had just figured by then I wasn't interested in nothing, which is what it would have been."

"You didn't like her?"

"No, I liked her a lot, but I didn't—I don't like friends for sex." He held her cheek. "I wanted a relationship with a woman who mattered. Who I knew cared. Who I cared for. I wanted to find that and move forward, see if we could make it last. That wasn't Janice."

She bit her lip and stared at him. "You slept with me."

He nodded a little. "I did notice that."

Her gaze dropped as the same fear etched into her gut. She wanted to believe him. History told her otherwise.

He leaned closer, whispering. "I picked out your tattoos and I know where I want them to go."

Her gaze came back up.

His hand moved soft across her arms, to her shoulder, leaving goose bumps. Fingers trailed down her back until she arched. He stopped between her shoulders, and made a circle. "Right here," he said. "I want to see it right here."

"What if I don't like ink?"

"Then you're in bed with the wrong guy because I'm a little marked up."

She licked her lips. "I like it on you. It's sexy."

"A rose," he said. "I looked online and found one I really like."

She watched him talk.

"It's a rose and it is encased by a heart. There's this really delicate chain, like it might be gold, pulling the two together. I think it's perfect for you."

"I become one of your roses?"

He kissed her on the nose. "You already did."

"You said two," she said.

He leaned over her to her night stand, opening the drawer and finding a fine tip Sharpie.

He popped the lid with his thumb and picked up her left hand.

He drew carefully, making the two inch infinite symbol on the base of her thumb, to the back of her hand, leaving one of the edges open.

He added a flowing TGM. *Trevor Martin Grant.*

He lifted her hand to his mouth and kissed the still damp drawing.

Turning to put his hand up, he repeated, trading out the initials with HLP. *Hannah Lynn Parker.*

He tossed the pen on the dresser topless. "That's temporary and I will touch it up every time it fades until we find someone with a needle gun to make it permanent."

"How can you be so sure?" she asked.

"Because I've been loved. By girlfriends, family, even Gavin. I know what it feels like and I know what it feels like to offer it back."

She still stared down.

"You never had that," he said, reaching up to hold her cheek in his hand. "I will help with that."

She smiled a little and looked at him. "I'm scared."

"That's okay. You can be scared. You let me take the lead for a while and when you catch up, let me know."

CHAPTER EIGHT

It took three years, two moves and a final descent into every day for her to catch up, but it was worth every minute of uncertainly and doubts to arrive in the place she had. The three of them made a team. What the two men felt for each other, they drew her in to be a part of their lives. Gavin held her close like she had never had…expect for Trevor, who held her closer.

Three blocks away from their apartment, an auto repair restoration shop, Judges & Outlaws, had a six month waiting list for American Muscle restoration.

Dinner at seven every night. She cooked, they groaned about their figures she was ruining.

"The Camaro only needed that front side done." Gavin said, as he dried his hands on paper towels, leaning his butt on the counter. "I almost have that finished. Should get paid in a couple of days. It's not a lot, but won't hurt."

The kitchen is where they would talk the business of their life. Her office, the third bedroom, is where she would pay the bills next Tuesday.

Trevor leaned back at the table, looking tired. "The Challenger is taking longer. A lot more wrong with it than we thought. Might be a few more weeks, but that check should keep us going awhile."

"Lease is up in three months," Hannah said. "We can buy a house with a garage at home. More space. Maybe a yard. Seemed to recall you two liked to dig pointless holes."

He grabbed her around the waist, pulling her into his lap while Gavin laughed.

"I'm fine here," Trevor said. "It's the nicest apartment we've ever had."

"Yeah," she said, with a smile. Three bedrooms, top floor near The Bay, might be the nicest she ever had, too.

"You want to think about moving though, we can think about moving."

She put her head on his shoulder. "Not sure. Let me think on it."

He kissed her and leaned over to whisper. "Feed us. We're starved."

It took another night for her sleeping beside him for her to finally face the fact she had been avoiding for almost a week.

She waited until they had gone to work then got her purchases.

Standing in the bathroom, Hannah stared at the stick with its plus sign and wondered how the hell she was going to work this out as part of life on the run.

Two other sticks sat on the counter with the same results, as if she took it enough times, there might be another answer.

She didn't have a clue how either of her men would react.

Gathering the evidence, she put them in the front pocket of her laptop case, knowing they would never check there.

Sinking down on their bed, she put her head in her hands and went through ten scenarios to tell him. Anyway she looked at it, on the run and baby didn't add up. Looking up, she saw her old friend, Future Frank, on her nightstand. She picked him up and shook him.

"How screwed am I?" she asked.

She shook him and turned him to look at his stomach. *"Your future is set."*

Three hours later they came home on schedule for the night, dirty, grimy and smelling of motor oil.

"Can I talk to you?" she asked, as Trevor leaned into the refrigerator.

He stood up with the beer, breathed heavy and twisted off the cap. "Can it wait a few minutes? I would love to get a shower and a few beers in me before I think too hard."

"Sure," she smiled. "It can wait."

He came forward, kissed her on the side of the mouth. "Work was totally fucked up. Everything went wrong and I am in a bitch of a mood. Can you give me a few to catch up and I will listen to anything?"

"Sure," she smiled. "And don't swear."

"When is dinner?"

"Lasagna. It's about done."

"Can you hold it long enough for me to grab a shower?"

She smiled and nodded and tried to push aside the panic of the upcoming conversation. She still didn't know what to say.

He was gone under ten minutes when she heard him from the master bath.

"God damn it."

She opened the door and he was yanking the towel off the rod, barely wet.

"There is no fucking hot water."

"Hey," she snapped.

"Not tonight, okay? I will fuck up and down all night long tonight and will not apologize once. Work was beyond a bitch. I will never get that fucking engine built back to standard." He wrapped the towel around his hips.

"I want four beers, one game and a good night's sleep."

"You'll do it," she smiled, sad. "You always do."

He moved into their bedroom and dropped the towel to a good view for her, then grabbed a pair of sweats, yanking them on, showing off his back-tat of roses.

His half smile still worked. She walked over to him, put her arms around his waist and kissed him deep. His mood settled some.

"I made a Dutch Apple Pie. Will that help?"

His arms went around her. "I smelled it when I walked in. We could skip dinner and go straight for the pie? Assuming you bought vanilla ice cream."

"I got chocolate," she teased.

He kissed her on the forehead, grabbed a T-shirt proclaiming 'Firefly Still Lived' and went to the kitchen and grabbed a beer.

They got to the living room and Gavin had the remote.

"I am not even going to tell you the game didn't record last night."

"That's probably a good idea," Trevor said. "I think there are still laws against what I might do."

She found a Jackie Chan movie that appeased them, made some popcorn and stood back to take care of her own. While they watched she kept herself busy on the computer. She sat at her computer while visiting sites that had not been on her agenda yesterday.

A website had a calculator giving her the ability to figure out a due date and she wondered what that would be like. He loved kids, he loved to go to the park three streets over and sit and watch them play on the equipment. He missed his brothers and sisters and cousins and seeing the kids always made him a little sad while offering some comfort.

He stood, heading toward the kitchen, coming by her on the way, kissing her on the neck and peeking over her shoulder.

"What are you working on?"

She had the website closed and Victoria's Secret open.

He looked at the screen. "I can get into this," he smiled.

She glanced at him.

He grabbed her hand and pulled her to her feet. His mood was back on track but the words in her mind 'tell him' didn't fit yet.

He got two beers, handing her one. She shook her head. "I'll take a root beer."

He made the exchange and dragged her back to the couch, sitting down, before pulling her next to him and pulling her tight.

She closed her eyes, loving the feel of him.

"Want to watch *A Princess Bride*?" he asked.

She looked at Gavin who nodded.

They watched, they laughed when they were supposed to and then the men went to bed. The shop opened at 7:30.

By the time she finished on the website ordering things that would only fit for a few months, she found him face down on the mattress, the bathroom light left on to give her enough light to move around.

Partially on his side, one arm raised above his head to disappear under the pillow, his hands curled in front of him. He was in his boxers.

She went to the bathroom, washed up and came back in and slid into the sheets carefully, trying not to disturb him.

He moved in his sleep, sliding the distance between them and pressing his chest to her back, his hand in front of her. She picked up his fingers, entwined them with hers and settled back against him.

She woke when he kissed her good-bye and she rolled onto her back.

"Do you want me to grab you something before I take off?"

She shook her head. "I don't feel good this morning."

He put a hand to her cheek. "You okay?"

"Probably. Just need to sleep some more."

He kissed her forehead. "I'll try to get home early. Maybe bring some take-out."

Feeling better but not enough to open the computer, Hannah got out of bed later than her usual sleep-in time. Still very aware of her circumstances, she decided to walk the two blocks to their favorite market. Perusing the aisles, her gaze locked on pre-natal vitamins. She walked past three times before deciding she might as well face the facts. She would tell him tonight, maybe after a walk.

If he was really okay with this idea.

She thought he would be okay with this idea.

She paid, dropped her purchase into her purse and moved down the street to Blackjack's Coffee House. More Starbucks than they would like to be, they had the same array of selections while offering light meals.

She took a chair outside, ordered a California omelet, extra avocado and a side of mango. She loved every bite. Avocado and mango, she had read last night, were good for her.

Pulling out her tablet, she opened a file that was on her list today when a shadow blocked out the sun.

She looked up and found a man she had never seen before standing over her.

"Hi," he smiled. "Do you mind if I sit here?"

Looking around the crowded café, she saw seating was limited and she would be done in a few minutes.

"That's fine," she said, looking back at her file.

Twelve-year old case. Thirteen-year old girl, found by the side of the road.

She hated these cases. Too young with too many things done to her. And they still needed a voice.

"Do you live around here?"

She looked up. He was staring at her. "Excuse me?" she asked him.

His eyes were an intense green, vivid in a face with little color. His head was shaved. Even his eyebrows were too thin to be natural.

And she didn't share personal information.

"No," she said. "Just visiting." She started loading up her belongings, when she heard him chuckle. He was staring at the bottle of vitamins visible in her open bag.

"Congratulations," he said, toasting with his coffee.

She put everything in her bag and stared at him three feet across from her. "Do you think I know you?"

"I think our paths have crossed when you weren't looking."

"I might remember that. Wanna give me a clue?"

"I've seen you here," he said. "And not alone. You have two friends you spend a lot of time with and I might want to get more information on that."

The word bounty hunter hit her mind but she didn't flinch.

"I have a lot friends. Like Deacon." While staring at this man, she called over her shoulder, loud. "Deacon?"

Quickly a heavy set man approached, smiling ear to ear. "Miss Hannah?"

Deacon came from small-town Georgia. Born and raised by a Mama who taught him to always be polite, it would never cross his mind to be anything but. He liked the community and non-judgmental atmosphere of San Francisco; it felt more comfortable for him. He was over six five, had weight to go with it and he liked his regulars.

"Deacon," she said. "I don't know this man, I don't want to know him and I would like you to help me out."

The smile slid away and Deacon's back straightened making him taller.

"You causing trouble with Miss Hannah?" Deacon asked in a southern drawl that turned tough. "You're not going to talk bad to anyone in my store."

"I wasn't causing trouble," he said. "I thought I knew Miss Hannah from somewhere and was trying to get reacquainted. No harm."

"You upset Miss Hannah, you upset me. How about you take your to-go cup somewhere else and not come back here."

"My apologies," he said. The smile said miles away from happy. The eyes, she took them into her memory and started sorting internal images. She had seen them. She didn't know where.

"Hannah," he tipped his hand to his head and left by the gate on the right.

She sat at the table trying to think fast. Her thoughts clogged by too much information. She weighed the possibility that someone could have found them.

"You okay Miss Hannah?"

"Do you mind if I sit here for a minute?"

"Where were you thinking of going?"

"Um," she looked up into his face. It was kind and gentle. "I wanted to walk over to the shop."

"Let me get the counter covered. I'll walk with you. Will that be nice?"

She smiled. She liked the people that had become friendly. She didn't want to put him out, but being alone right seemed—something wasn't setting. "If it's not any trouble, yeah, I think the company would be nice."

They had four or five places they liked to have lunch that weren't too far to walk from Judges & Outlaws. Today it was sandwiches. Ham and cheese on sourdough, though to this day, no sandwich had ever tasted as good as the one on the hood of that car in the forest all those years ago.

"How's Sally?" Trevor smirked as he ate his chips.

"Why do you always bring that up?"

"Because you're more cheerful when you're getting some fun and not sneaking cat food out the door."

Gavin was feeding a feral cat and liked to pretend his hard ass wasn't.

Gavin smiled. "Sally likes cats."

"What else does Sally like?"

"I'll give up details if you will," Gavin laughed.

"Ah huh, and then when she makes her tacos for you, you can smile and try to keep a straight face and not picture us—"

"Stop." Gavin's hand came up. "Point taken."

Trevor smiled and picked up his sandwich. He looked up and saw Hannah walking toward their table. She stopped, kissed Deacon on the cheek and started toward them. Deacon waved then headed back.

"Wow," he grinned. "Nice surprise. Why was Deacon with you?"

Standing, he kissed her and took her hand to help her to the table.

"He was out and about."

"With his apron on?"

She glanced at him then away.

"Surprise," Gavin said. He shifted his bag of potato chips in her direction.

"Do you want something?" Trevor asked, motioning to the menu. "You can have half of this," he said, "and I'll get you a drink."

"No, I'm fine," she said, picking up his cup of soda and taking a suck on the straw. She put it down and made a face.

"Are you still not feeling good?" he asked her.

She looked at him. "I think I ate something icky."

He didn't stop worrying about her.

"Want me to pick up something on the way home? Nyquil or something?"

"No, that's okay. Bed earlier tonight."

She rested her folded hands on the table, and she looked just this side of herself, as if it was more than something she ate. The way her hands sat, he could see the inch and half tattoo on the back of her left hand, near the thumb...a match to the one on his left hand.

She looked at them, then back to the table, before looking back up.

"Hannah?" he asked, setting his sandwich down to stare at her.

She looked at him.

"I just had a very strange encounter with a very strange man."

"What do you mean?" Trevor asked.

"What did he say?" Gavin asked, sitting forward.

"He knew who I was," she said. "He knew I was acquainted with two men. He didn't say anything direct but it spooked me enough to think about looking for alternate zip codes."

"What was his name?"

"He didn't tell me. He didn't say much other than what I said."

"So he might have seen you, wanted a pick up?"

She looked at him. "Maybe."

"Or he is a bounty hunter," Gavin said, "and our life just got a whole lot more complicated."

"I did think of that," she said.

"What are you thinking now?"

She looked at Trevor. "I think we should plan a long talk tonight."

He sat against the chair back. "Are you okay?"

She nodded. Her skin was still a little pale and she didn't have the look of '*I got this*' but she didn't look off the charts either.

"Deacon walked me over," she said.

"From Blackjack's? It was that bad?"

"I don't know," she said, looking at him. "It sort of made me nervous, I guess," she said, with a small smile.

"Why don't I take you home? Make sure everything is okay."

"I can take care of the shop," Gavin said.

"No," she said, tilting her head. "I don't think it's that serious. Besides I have to stop by the farmers market for dinner. You'd lose a half day's work."

"I don't mind. Do you mind?" he asked Gavin.

Gavin shrugged. "Not at all. Give me a chance for a non-hostile take-over and seduce all the girls."

Trevor smiled at the attempt to lighten the mood. "Annie. You're going to seduce our fifty-seven year old receptionist?"

"I'm desperate," he said, finishing his chips and rolling up the bag.

"If you guys don't mind, I'm going to do a little looking around. See what I put together about our position."

"Looking around," Gavin laughed. "That means something completely different for you than the rest of the world."

She looked down shyly and smiled.

"You're breaking out the brain," Trevor said.

She smiled. "I do want to talk later tonight about something unrelated, if that's okay."

"Is everything alright?"

"I just need a few minutes."

Trevor looked at Gavin who shrugged. Trevor looked back at her. "If you don't want me to take you home, I'll be there about 6:30."

She stood up, leaning over to kiss Gavin on the cheek, making him smile. Trevor was standing when she came around the table. He put a hand on her lower back and did a little bit better job than Gavin. When she walked away, they both watched.

"Do you have a plan?" Gavin asked.

"It's a work in progress."

Gavin chuckled. "You do realize there are only a few subjects a woman in our circumstances would want to talk to you about privately tonight and I'm not thinking she overdrew your mutual checking account."

Trevor looked at him. "Had crossed my mind."

"Got any opinions on that?"

"Do you think I would have an opinion that might shock you?"

Gavin smiled wide and leaned back, folding his hands on his stomach. "Fucking took you two long enough."

Trevor stared at him. "How long did you know? About me and her?"

Gavin stared at him. "Since you read your Snapple lid in the forest, which I guess was the best Snapple you ever had, right up there with your ham sandwich. Cuz my sandwich rocked. What did the lid say anyway?"

Trevor worked his jaw, looked away. "Slugs have four nostrils."

Gavin laughed. "And where is it?"

Trevor paused, feeling the embarrassment on his face. "Sock drawer."

"You're going steady with a Snapple lid."

Hannah took her time at the farmer's market. She was making a stir fry tonight and needed a fresh assortment of vegetables. She went to the butcher and got the beef. Taking a few minutes, she got a little snack at a café and pulled out her tablet, firing it up and searched the Internet.

They didn't have many hard and set rules. Safety sat #1.

It was agreed that if one felt their security had been compromised, the other two would not argue. Changes would be made.

She loved San Francisco. The smells of the city, the sounds. The top floor apartment they shared was way overpriced but they had a view of The Bay with Alcatraz in the distance.

Coming up the street, her cloth bag on her shoulder, her oversized purse, the knot in her gut grew. There were too many things to talk about tonight.

She came up the inside stairwell that led them to the top floor. If they ever did get a place of their own, she might think about those two kitten's Gavin had once suggested. Right now, the no pet rule kept them pet less.

She came into the apartment, down the hall and froze as she came into the dining room, her weight shifting, her back straight.

He was sitting at the far end of the table. The man from Blackjacks. She sucked in a breath and took a step back. Running didn't cross her mind. He had his hand on the cocked revolver at his fingertips. She couldn't outrun bullets.

Body hair, she thought. He was shaved. He couldn't leave trace evidence if he didn't have body hair.

In his other hand, he held a switchblade, open. He was spinning the blade into the table making a hole.

"I didn't introduce myself before," he said, standing. She took another step back and dropped the groceries and her purse. Colorful vegetables scattered around her feet.

"My name is Simon Brenner. I think you knew my dad. Well, you knew *about* my dad. You destroyed everything he ever was."

CHAPTER NINE

They were back in the shop for an hour when concentration became almost impossible. Instead of goofing off with the Challenger, Trevor really needed to get home and talk to Hannah about whatever she needed to talk to him about.

He tried to focus and not to think what he was thinking, because there *was* a list of other options. She talked occasionally about buying a house. Not enough to start packing but enough to make him think that might be it.

He liked the image he was thinking better. God, take her current gorgeous, add the rest and he would be laid level by her mere presence. He smiled as he pulled the speedometer.

In the background the radio played the sixties rock while Gavin worked on his project and Trevor moved around on his, never actually accomplishing anything.

Judges & Outlaws, named by his clever girlfriend, did its share of jobs. But they kept their operation small on purpose. Less projects, less attention.

Annie came in, carrying basic office supplies that didn't tax her. She wasn't in great shape for fifty-seven but she made great coffee. She came by Trevor like a thousand times before but this time she lost her grip on what she was carrying, the box fell to the ground right in front of Trevor, snapping and breaking as glass escaped the cardboard packaging.

Trevor stood up stiff to stare down at the mess.

Light bulbs.

Annie had been carrying a dozen containers of light bulbs.

She was on her knees, trying to make the mess manageable while Trevor stood frozen.

"I stocked up because they were on sale. I'm sorry, Mr. Galban."

That mild feeling of uncertainly he was trying to pretend wasn't there, started again.

Box by box he had unloaded that fucking flat while his Mom lay already dead. No cops had come to tell him. No notification. By the time he got home that morning, the bodies were being loaded in the coroners van. They were gone and nothing but yellow tape was left and a house that needed a thorough cleaning.

He and Gavin had never spent another night in their home.

He wasn't heavy into ghost stories but one morning when Gavin had been asleep, Trevor was having cereal alone in the studio apartment they shared. It hadn't even been a year yet when he could smell his mom's perfume. It wasn't expensive but she never went without and he was positive that he wasn't alone. Goosebumps had risen on his arms.

Two weeks later he had woken from a dream of happier times with happy faces and felt someone sitting on the edge of his bed.

Nothing had been there, but it was all day before he shook the feeling he wasn't alone.

He wouldn't do anything to put Hannah in danger. But his gut told him that he may have put her somewhere she shouldn't be.

He looked up at Gavin who watched him from his project.

"Do you hear that?"

"The Beatles," Gavin said.

"*My Life*," Trevor said, putting two and two together in something impossible. "Mom's favorite song."

Three of the overhead light bulbs exploded in a spark that had everyone covering their heads.

When Trevor stood straight, he whispered a soft, "Hannah."

Turning sharply, he ran to the office, dropping to the large black safe. When that opened, he pulled out the smaller safe, entered in the code that only he and Gavin had and pulled out his 9mm. Hannah still hated guns, so they kept them here.

"What?" Gavin asked from the door.

Trevor looked at him, feeling his own body shake.

"Close up shop. Follow me. Hurry."

Sweat edged into his eyes from the three block sprint, crossing the streets in what had to be record time while feeling like it took forever.

The key in the door while his hands shook.

He entered carefully, both hands on the butt of the gun. Her cloth bag was on the floor, just in the edge of the hall, vegetables spilled. He blew out a breath, understood life and death happened and he came out on top.

The laughter coming from the dining room wasn't hers.

The small sobs, those were hers.

Trevor swung into the room, the gun up. The man had her slammed against the wall, a revolver to her head. Trevor didn't have time for the shot he would gladly take and with that gun where it was, this was going to be tricky.

He could see her shaking hard, the shortness of breath. Her wrists were bound with duct tape, the back of her hand, bloody. Her left eye was swelling shut to match the red marks on her face. He didn't know where all the blood came from but figured real quickly any amount was too much.

"She said you left for work."

"I did," Trevor said, gun aimed. "I realized I forgot something valuable. I came back for it. You want to let it go?"

"I'm going to kill her no matter what. Hoped to have some time with that. Spraying her brains on the wall while you watch works for me, too."

"And that gets you a bounty?"

The man looked a little confused. "She doesn't have a bounty. She creates them." Then he seemed to get it. "But *you* have a bounty," he said, "right? Interesting." He laughed a little more. "The great detective keeps criminal company. Someone will surely like to hear about that."

Trevor held the gun steady and calculated. He had the shot, if he fired first. If she wasn't there.

"He's going to kill you, Simon Brenner," she whispered, sounding as if it was hard to talk.

"No, that just means I have to kill him, too, since now he knows who I am."

"No, he will," she whispered.

Trevor could see it. The only thing holding her up was this asshole's hands.

And this bastard wasn't taking Hannah. That was a fact written somewhere in the universe.

"If he tries to kill me," Simon said softly in her ear. "Then the last thing I will see is his face as I take the two of you from him."

Her gaze dropped, her breathing heavy and he knew now what he had hoped was true.

Trevor's head came up a little, the angle not as pronounced for the shot. He let out a hard breath.

"They walk?" Trevor asked. "I will turn myself in if they walk."

"Yeah, sure. Honor and shit."

Trevor took a deep breath, let it out and flexed his shoulders.

"Trevor, no," she said, staring at him. He smiled at her, ready to see this through if he couldn't pull it off.

"I know what he's done," she said. "He won't stop if you are gone."

Laughing a little, he had to take a chance, take a chance the bastard would alter the stand-off. Trevor dropped his arms with the weapon still in his hand, finger still on the trigger. His arms came away from his body in surrender. She was smart. She would figure it out.

Simon smiled. He tried to turn the gun and Trevor knew the other man was going to fire.

But she was watching.

Buckling her knees, gravity held more strength than this bastard's grip. Her whole body dropped to the floor in front of him, robbing Simon of his shot and handing Trevor his.

Simon tried to win. He fired to the floor toward Hannah.

Then Simon lost his head.

Charging around the table, Trevor grabbed Simon by the legs, dragging him off her. She was unconscious and blood smeared her head.

He ran into the kitchen for a dish towel and sat her up, putting pressure on the towel on the side of her head, high, above the temple. Checking, he saw it was only an inch long. It would bleed like a bitch, but she would be okay.

"Honey, come on. Say something," he said, cupping her cheek with the other hand. He brushed a thumb over her swollen lower lip.

"Hannah," he said, louder. "Come on."

She blinked hard, but still out of focus. Her hand came up to hold his wrist. She looked at him and didn't say anything.

Footsteps came down the hall and Trevor was around on his knee, the gun ready.

Gavin came in armed.

Trevor lowered his weapon and turned toward her.

"I think you might have had a more interesting afternoon than I did," Gavin said,

"She had it worse. I'm not sure she's here yet." He cut the duct tape from her wrists finding her skin red and raw.

"That's a fucking lot of blood," Gavin said.

"Don't swear," she whispered.

Trevor smiled. "Good girl." He picked up her hand, looking at the slice on the back of her ring finger. It was deep but not stitches deep.

"Tickets," she whispered, holding on to his hand.

"What tickets?"

"Farmer's Market. Bought boat tickets out. Didn't feel safe."

"Smart girl," he said, touching her face, feeling her alive. That was good, he sighed. He couldn't do roses to another grave.

"Pier 42. *Talisman*. Leaves at one a.m."

Her cries started softly, her hand covering her face. He reached over, slid his arms under her knees and back, lifted her and carried her to the bed in their room.

He held her tight until the crying stopped, feeling his own eyes damp. Using a home first aid kit, he looked her over; pulling off the clothes she had been wearing, tossing them on the floor to be left. He pulled out a change of clothes, soft, sweet smelling sweats and a T-shirt that had the word 'LOVERS' stacked in block lettering. He had bought it for her by The Bay.

"How bad?" he asked her.

She kept her gaze down. There were slices and cuts on her arms. He leaned in close, holding her face. "You have to tell me, Hannah. I can't help if you don't tell me."

Her gaze still down. "No," she whispered. "But he made me watch him..." her eyes dropped and she made an obscene gesture with her hand. "I know his work." Her eyes closed. "It's how he starts."

Fury, more profound than he thought possible, hit his nerves.

"He was going to..." she took a breath and stopped. "...he was going to but thought he had hours. You came home. Why did you come home?"

"I think my Mom wanted me to," he smiled, tight.

She looked at him. "What?"

"I will explain later. Do you think everyone is okay?"

She looked at him.

"I can take you to an ER. Get an ultrasound or something."

She shook her head a little, a tear slipping. "He was careful. Wanted to save that for last."

"You know who he was?"

"I busted his father about six months ago. A serial killer in South Dakota. I got the father. I didn't know the son was part of it. He used to go with him and help. He thought I was going to bust him, too."

He closed his eyes. In the end when caught, it was her job and not theirs that almost destroyed them all.

"Trevor," Gavin said from the door.

Trevor's gaze darted.

"I need to talk to you a minute."

Trevor expected a subdued Gavin right now, he didn't expect the tremor to Gavin's voice or the pale face.

He cupped her cheek. "One minute, okay?"

She nodded.

Gavin moved out of the doorway into the hallway. Trevor had to turn to follow.

"What? I'm sorta busy."

Gavin held up a black backpack Trevor had not seen before. He looked at Gavin.

"It was in the chair by the table." Gavin opened the zipper and pulled it open. "Whoever he is, I don't think he got through airport security and I don't think he was after any bounty."

Trevor took the edge of the bag and pulled, peering inside.

There was a roll of duct tape, pair of pliers. As Trevor's hands began to shake and his breath became shallow, he reached in and pulled out five unopened guitar strings. He held them as not to leave finger prints. He dropped them back in; saw the box of razors, another gun and the most horrifying thing of all, an altered dildo in a size he never knew existed.

He stared in the bag, his voice trapped.

"Front pocket," Gavin said. "Don't look. They're photos. In this city. You can see The Bay and the Bridge. She wasn't his first."

Trevor looked to the open door to the living room. "We're all over this place. Finger prints, hairs." He looked at Gavin. "CSI comes in here and we'll be tagged within the hour. They tag us, they find out about her."

"Trace evidence," Gavin managed a smile. She always tried to warn them about trace evidence.

"We have to call this in. He can't disappear. There are others out there. Victims. Too many cold cases."

"We walk," Gavin said.

Trevor liked that Gavin said it and didn't ask. "She told me. She bought tickets."

"Where?"

"Didn't say. Start packing and order a cab for sooner rather than later. I'll get her ready. We'll call it after we are clear."

"We walk away from the projects. Start over?"

Trevor looked at him, not seeing humor or sarcasm in Gavin. They had shifted into the doorway and Gavin's gaze was on her. It didn't take an over abundance of IQ to register what almost happened here, what they almost lost.

"I'm thinking since there is a dead man in our dining room, I think wherever that boat is heading might have cars that need our help."

Gavin managed a smile. "We keep ours safe."

"Order the taxi," Trevor said. He didn't care how early they were to the docks; he wanted to get away from the body in the other room. Sheet or no sheet coving him, the bastard stayed behind.

Trevor got her sunhat out of the closet along with a pretty colorful scarf around her neck and added the sunglasses.

Emergency exits were always a possibility. One suitcase each, Future Frank, her personal stuff and the computer. Always the computer.

"Taxi's here," Gavin called.

San Francisco had been home, the home they built together. When they came to the curb with their bags, Hannah's step flattering, Trevor opened the back door of the taxi and knew as much as it hurt to loose here, there was a there waiting.

They left their lease on the apartment, the shop and The Judge.

That first night in the forest, she had warned them: *life on the run*.

This is what it looked like.

CHAPTER TEN

They got to the gangplank, a Hispanic man helped take the bags and Trevor was able to concentrate on her, his arm around her, helping her past the shock he would deal with in a room.

At the top, a dark expansion of deck ran in either direction.

"Who the hell are you?"

"We booked rooms," Trevor said. "Name's probably Parker, but we have choices."

"Two rooms?" the man asked. "What's wrong with you?"

She looked up at him. "Stairs. I fell."

"You fell down some stairs? *Vraiment?*" Really?

"The rooms," Trevor said.

"*Attendez ici.*" The man turned to go while another pulled a gun.

"He said to wait here," she said.

Trevor kept a hand on her arm, but felt her sinking lower. Gavin took the other side, helping to hold her up. Too many minutes ticked by.

"Oh, fuck this," Trevor said, he took ten steps toward a crate, while Mr. Gun threatened him.

"What the fuck do you think you're doing?"

Trevor froze with his hands on the wood. "Go ahead and shoot. That will help."

He carried the crate back, sat it down behind her. It was low, but he helped her sink onto it and crutched down beside her. "Can you hold on a few more minutes?"

"I'm fine," she said.

Three men came forward, armed. Trevor stood straight, one side inching a little to stand in front of her. Gavin took the other.

"You two will back up," the man obviously in change said.

They looked at each other and didn't move.

"You will do more for her dead because they will shoot and you will die. We only have to go twenty miles out to sea before we toss you over."

"Shit," Gavin muttered.

They took three steps back, their teeth grinding.

The gun shifted to her.

"We paid for rooms," Trevor snapped. "This is how we travel?"

The Captain took a few steps forward. He pulled the hat and scarf off, and put a finger under her chin to see the side of her face.

"Stairs?"

"It's a better story than reality so yeah, I'll stick with it."

"Did either of these men do this to you?"

She pointed over her left shoulder. "That is my boyfriend of three years." She pointed over the right. "That is his cousin who is my big brother."

"And in my experience neither of those definitions excludes a man from doing this to his woman."

Her gaze snapped up.

"Then I think you hang out with bad men because my men wouldn't do this. They were out of the house, someone came in. Trevor and Gavin got back in time."

The Captain looked at her.

She pointed to the left. "Trevor." She pointed to the right. "Gavin. And they would throw themselves on a hand-grenade to stop this from happening to me."

Taking a deep breath she stood up to face him head on.

"Honey, sit," Trevor whispered.

Which she ignored.

"C'est moi avec qui vous traites. Pas eux." The Captain stared at her. "Asseyez-vous avant de tomber, madam."

"Give us our rooms and I will."

"Vous etes emmerdente."

"Yes, I am a pain in your ass. And I will be even more, I promise."

"That is your story?"

"My story is I spent $25,000 booking two rooms to get us far away from trouble. Now you either hand over the keys to those rooms or you let us walk away so we can make other plans, because what goes on in our lives really is none of your business."

The Captain looked at her then looked at Trevor. "You tamed this?"

"Wouldn't even if I could."

The Captain looked back to her. "You paid $10,000 for the rooms which are three times what they go for."

"And that bag by Gavin's feet is my computer. Give me three minutes on it and I can make all your dreams come true."

"She's not lying," Trevor said. "I would prefer she didn't but she can and she will ignore me if I ask her to stop."

The Captain looked her up and down. "That is Stefan behind me. He will take you to the rooms. We aren't a luxury liner, but they are nice and clean and comfortable. I will have your bags brought to you. Get her settled. I would like to hear about the stairs."

Trevor got the door open to their room while Gavin watched. Trevor stepped back to let Hannah enter.

Hannah headed straight for the bathroom, closing the door behind her.

"Can you wait in your room?" Trevor asked Gavin.

"Do you need anything?"

"Prayer?"

Gavin managed a chuckle then let himself into the room across the hall.

Trevor knocked on the bath door with his knuckles. He could hear the sounds and walked in before she said yes.

She was on her knees in front of the toilet, the smell a little overpowering. Placing her bag by the sink, he took the edge of the tub and rubbed her back.

He didn't know which was causing it. Shock, fear or…her not feeling well this week.

Reaching over he got a glass of water and pulled a towel closer.

He sank down beside her. "Here," he said softly, putting the glass to her mouth. "Swish and spit. It might help." He dug out the toothpaste, putting a smear on his finger, putting it near her mouth. She licked it off.

She fell back against the wall, her ass on the tiles.

She didn't want to talk so he pulled her bag closer, pulled out Future Frank and held it up for her to take.

"Ask him a question," he whispered, rubbing her hair.

"Did that really happen?" She whispered, before hugging Frank close.

Trevor had done bad things to bad men. He never hurt someone for sport, or whatever reason that man had come after her.

He looked at her. She was watching him.

"It's going to be a memory, Hannah. Pretty soon, a distant one. We all got out and we are safe here."

"You know that for sure?"

"I think so. I'm not going to promise that, but that is what we are going for. You okay to stand? I can get you into bed."

She nodded and he took hold of both her hands and pulled her to her feet. He helped her to the bed, positioned the pillows on the headboard and let her sit.

He finally sat on the edge of the bed near her, still for the first time, and clasped his hands in front of him and caught his first breath.

"You're mad?" she whispered from the top of the bed, where she leaned on the headboard.

He glanced in her direction then back into the room. "You didn't tell me. I had to hear from him."

"I didn't get a chance. I was going to last night and then everything went wrong. You were grouchy. By the time I got to bed you were asleep."

"You could have told before I went to work after lunch."

"I was going to tell you. I was trying to think of a special way that you would remember."

He laughed bitterly. "I think you did that part."

"I was thinking of the park. Watching the kids. You like to do that and I thought that would be a good time."

"You stepped in front of a gun and put not only yourself, but my child in danger." He looked at her.

"No I didn't. All I did was fall."

"He had a gun to your head."

"Not when I moved. You're mad at me for this?"

He chuckled. "Am I mad for something we were doing together that resulted in something unexpected that will no doubt bring us both joy for the rest of our lives?"

"Are you?"

"How did he know? Why is it he knew before me?" He was looking at her.

"Prenatal vitamins. He saw them in my purse while I was at Blackjacks."

"That might do it."

"Front pocket of the laptop case," she whispered.

He looked at the case then back at her.

"Front pocket," she said,

He paused and then moved to retrieve the sticks. He sat down beside her and fanned the sticks. "Three?" he smiled.

"I wanted to be sure."

He put two on the end table and held the last one toward her. "I don't know how to read this."

She took it and turned it over to show the window. "The straight line means negative and the plus sign means positive."

He looked at it with pursed lips and he nodded his head. "That's a pretty big plus sign."

He looked at her. "You were afraid to tell me?"

She shook her head. "Not afraid. I didn't think you would mind, I didn't know how and then hell broke loose."

He leaned toward her to kiss her, pushing her back into the headboard. "She is going to have long dark hair, big brown eyes and a rich life that ties me right around her little finger, just like her mom."

Trevor knocked on the door. It opened almost at once.

"God damn it. Could you have taken any longer? I almost went over ten times."

Trevor took the offered bottle of tequila, not even caring where it came from. He drank straight from the neck.

"I had to get her settled."

"Is she okay?" Gavin asked.

"No. I doubt she'll ever be okay."

Trevor sank into a chair with the bottle, drinking more. "She's asleep."

"Is that a good idea?"

"She says it's okay and I trust that she read it someplace."

Trevor handed the bottle back, then waited his turn. Gavin took a long drink then looked at him.

"What happened at the shop? How did you know to go home?"

"I think I was supposed to."

"You don't believe in that shit."

"No, I don't. But I will take it tonight and say thank you. The dead guy still on our floor? He was the son of one of Hannah's cold cases, one she finished about six months ago. Only it turned, what he told her tonight, dad and son used to work together. Dad died, but this guy was still active. He was afraid Hannah would figure it out."

"Fuck."

"Don't swear," Trevor almost smiled leaning back in the seat to close his eyes, his mind replaying every scene over again.

"I think I'm going to get married," he said, soft.

"I never knew why you waited."

"Never thought I needed to. She wasn't ever going anywhere."

"Seeing her sliced and diced made it cross your mind?"

"I think sea captains can marry couples. I thought I would ask him tomorrow. See if he'll do that."

Gavin held the bottle.

Trevor rolled his tongue in his cheek, reached in his back pocket and tossed the stick, Gavin caught it, looked at it, brought his gaze up to Trevor's then looked back.

"Did she wash this when she was done?"

Trevor chuckled. "I actually didn't ask her."

"And I have no idea how to read this but I'm thinking this is what she wanted to talk to you about."

"She found out yesterday. Things weren't exactly going well so she waited only things got a lot worse."

Gavin rolled the stick in his fingers, his lips pursed.

"What about Sally?" Trevor asked.

"What about her?"

"You have to walk away."

Gavin thought. "Sally was great, but it wasn't serious. I'll send her a note or something to smooth it over and see if she will go grab Felix."

Trevor looked at him. "Who the hell is Felix?"

"My cat," Gavin grinned. "I liked that bastard."

CHAPTER ELEVEN

Though the lights were still on when he got back, she was asleep. He thought that might be more needed than anything.

He watched her for a moment, thinking of life twists that had brought him here when he should have been in a six by eight barred cell with a toilet in view of the guards. Up at five for count and breakfast. Work crews, guards, guards and more guards. Food served on a tray, eaten with several hundred of his besties.

He should be there now instead of sleeping beside a beautiful woman expecting his child. He turned off all the lights.

He pulled off his clothes, and let them drop to the ground before sliding in next to her.

She settled further into the pillow and sighed only a little when he pressed his chest against her back, his arm wrapping around her, holding the love of his life close in a way he never dreamed.

She slept in his T-shirt and panties, as always. Sliding his hand along her stomach, he took it below her belly button, and rested his hand on her, his eyes closed, the small smile evident even to him.

When he concentrated, he could feel it. He was sure. There was a heat there that hadn't been there before, an energy that made him feel excited.

He leaned toward Hannah. "Are you asleep?" he whispered, watching her face. She didn't respond.

Lifting the blankets, he inched his way under until he was close enough to really appreciate his new life.

"Hey," he whispered softly, talking to her tummy. "I'm your daddy. I wanted to let you know I can't wait to meet you in person, Lacey."

He felt the blankets lift higher and he raised his gaze with an embarrassed grin.

"What are you doing?" she asked with a smile. The bruises had come in, the swelling too.

"I thought you were asleep."

"I was asleep. Something woke me up."

He rubbed her middle with his palm. "I was just saying hi."

"You smell like tequila."

"I had a shot," he grinned.

"I think you had half a bottle."

"Gavin got the worm."

"Good for Gavin. You know Lacey is a terrible name for a boy."

"Naw," he smiled wide, touching her more. "This is a girl. I'm sure of it. She's going to be beautiful like her mom and she is going to make her grandma proud."

Lacey was his Mom's name.

"I was thinking if it is a boy we might go with Jayce."

Jayce was his fifteen year old brother's name.

He slid up from under the blankets until he was over her. Her legs wrapped around one of his, trapping him.

"How drunk are you?" she asked, rubbing his back.

"Pretty," he admitted, leaning in to kiss her thoroughly, his fingers curling around her hurt cheek. "My girlfriend got hurt and I killed a man. I actually don't like doing that and tequila makes it more acceptable. I think."

"I'm sorry that happened. You do not need any more nightmares."

"The nightmare would have been if I had been late. I think my Mom wanted to make sure I got to meet my daughter."

"You don't believe in that."

"Tonight I do." He pulled back. "I don't tell you enough. I don't think I can tell you enough. I love you."

"You tell me every day."

"It's not enough," he whispered.

"What?"

"I don't know how to seduce you like this. I don't know what is acceptable."

She smiled. "I think for now, anything you want to do is fine though we may have to check and see in a few months. The biggest problem now is how much of that tequila you had and if you will remember this in the morning."

He kissed her hard, pushing her further into the mattress, holding her face. "I had enough. Not too much." He reached down to the hem of the T-shirt she wore, pulling it up and over her head.

"I think I will remember just fine."

CHAPTER TWELVE

Trevor walked to the table, waiting a second before the Captain's gaze came up to him.

"Do you have a minute?" Trevor asked.

The Captain motioned to the seat across with his hand. Trevor sat while the Captain leaned back in his chair.

"I wanted to ask if you could marry people."

"Are you thinking that you might need this service?" he asked in his French accent.

Trevor kind of nodded. "Yeah, I was thinking of it."

"She's beautiful. A little banged up, but beautiful."

Trevor wasn't sure the tone set well but he kept his face straight. "Thank you."

"How long have you been together?"

"Over three years."

"And you need to get married on the voyage? It makes a difference?"

Trevor shrugged a little. "Yeah. I think this time it does."

The Captain leaned forward in his seat. "I will tell you what. I will tell you if I can do this, if you can explain this to me."

He reached up and turned his laptop so that Trevor was staring at today's headline on Google News.

Gang Terror in the Streets: Man found executed in Glenwood Street Apartment

Trevor's gaze came up. "Violence in this town is a bitch. Can't get away from it."

"Except," The Captain said, "that wasn't gang. One shot. No other bullets fired, no excess damage...if you want to debate what excess damage can translate to."

"I guess that will depend. Did you say you could marry us?"

"Your girl, I spoke to her for five minutes and even I can tell you she's highly educated."

"Don't play *Trivial Pursuit* with her."

"Probably well off for how she paid for these rooms, protective of her companions, who if run their first names as a pair through the right search engine you can get a hit, even if the last names are different. Are you fond of 80's vampire movies?"

Trevor leaned back in the chair, pursed his lips and folded his hands over his middle. Things took a sharp turn from bad to worse when all he wanted was make his girl honorable.

There were a couple of ways to go and he seriously doubted pulling a con on this guy would work.

"Actually I always thought it was a pretty stupid tag. You going to turn us in?"

"It seems it would be more profitable for me not to. Even my offshores are suddenly gathering an interest rate I hadn't expected."

"She does things like that."

"And you carry a gun with a silencer?"

"I *have* a gun with a silencer, yes. I don't generally carry it."

"The blood on her hand."

"He was trying to cut off her ring finger."

"The cuts on her arms?"

"Who the fuck knows. I don't think tact was his first language."

"You knew him?"

"No, but she did. In her work. She's a cold case detective. He thought he would take her out before she took him out."

"How did a middle class working man like you end up with a highly educated class act who has more in one account then you will make in a life time?"

Trevor leaned forward and paused. "You know, I don't have a clue." He laughed, giving up. "I have tried to figure that out. She had a thousand options but she settled for me. I cannot figure it out and I never ask."

"Why do you not ask?"

"Because if I did, she might wake up and realize what a mistake she made. I like her where she is."

"Standing behind you?" The Captain smiled.

Trevor turned and smiled up at her. "Hey, you're supposed to be asleep."

"Gavin said you were off doing wicked things."

"Just want to keep you honest," he smiled.

She sat down on his knee and leaned into him.

"Do we have a problem?" she asked the Captain.

"I have not decided, though there was another five thousand in my account this morning."

"Funny about that," she said. "And I think that will continue to happen as long as I have internet connection."

"Do you know the names of the men you travel with?"

"I *created* the names of the men I travel with. And I don't really think that concerns you."

"How do you figure?"

"You're honorable, loyal. You are willing to put up a lot as long as it feeds your greed, which you also love. I looked you up."

"The price on their head—"

"There isn't a price on my head as I am not on record of ever doing anything. But if you want to compare what it could be to what I have sitting in one bank in New York and can transfer to you in a heartbeat, we can talk."

"No," the Captain said, smiling.

"No what?" she asked.

"I was answering your boyfriend's question. I cannot marry anyone."

"You can't what?" she asked.

"But we are picking up a group of missionaries with some cargo in San Diego. One is a priest. I know they struggle. A donation might help them."

She turned in Trevor's lap to stare at him.

He smiled sneaky, feeling the guilt. "I was going to ask real nice."

The ceremony was simple. No fancy clothes and enough of her limited make-up to take the marks on her face down a bit. She was still the most beautiful woman he had ever seen, and the words left him short of breath.

"Do you take her? I will."

"Do you take him? I will."

The rings were made of steel, forged to size by one of the engine room men.

Gavin standing close, Father Simpson accepted his fat donation and smiled, proclaiming them man and wife.

"You lose," Gavin said straight-faced

Trevor turned to him.

"The park. We were about fifteen, sixteen. I bet you ten bucks you would do it before me so now you have to pay up."

"How drunk was I?"

"You tried to make out with a tree. I think. I was pretty wasted, too."

"I'm keeping my ten," Trevor laughed.

Gavin moved past Trevor to wrap his arm around her lower back, pulling her gently toward him, planting a heavy kiss on her, without hurting her. When he let go, Trevor slapped him on the back of the head with a "hey" while she giggled.

"I didn't get one in the forest," he grinned. "And I imagine I won't be getting another chance." His smile was wide.

The reception was as simple as the ceremony and Hannah was just as happy.

A group gathered in the mess with something that looked like a cake the cook had managed. Crew came and went until just the five of them were left.

Gavin, Trevor, his bride with the Captain and first mate, Curt.

"You have a diverse crew," Trevor said. "From all over the world."

"*Qui*," he said. "Curt is from Portugal. We have a Russian. Even some from America. It seems everyone wants to escape something."

"What did you escape?" Gavin asked.

"Boredom." He looked at Hannah. "Beautiful lady," André, the Captain, smiled. "What you did for your men — you started where most people end."

She smiled. "I smoked pot in college."

He laughed. "Anything else?"

"*Non*," she said. "I never had the need."

André smiled. "What lengths would you go to protect these men?"

With a glass of French wine in front of each of them and a ginger-ale in front of her, she smiled at him, her chin down, her gaze up. "I think that might be one of those questions best left undiscovered."

CHAPTER THIRTEEN

With the sea sickness adding to a stomach already queasy, she accepted the kiss good morning, rolled over and heard the promise of breakfast in bed when they came back.

Asleep for a while with unsettling dreams, it took some time for her to realize the *'when they came back'* part never happened.

The clock said it was almost noon and, sitting up in the bed, she knew this wasn't right.

She got up and she grabbed the computer and checked the ships schedule, its arrival times and its crews.

In less than two minutes she saw the miscalculated error she had made. It was an error so severe, it could be fatal. She snapped the lid shut and ran, not walked. There was no way in hell for it to be that small a world.

She hit the bridge, her heart pounding, all attention was out of the window in front.

André turned to smile at her. "Madame," he said.

She stepped further into the room. "What is happening?"

"We are heading into port."

"How long," she asked.

"An hour, maybe."

She scratched her upper lip then moved further into the room.

Curt stood to the right, two other officers looking busy.

She leaned close to André and whispered. "You have a man onboard. His name is Joseph Williams."

"*Qui*. Yes. He works in our engine room. He made your rings."

Feeling sick with that knowledge, she smiled and said, "*Merci*," and turned to leave.

He gently grabbed her by the arm. "You are white."

"I have to go to the engine room."

"*Pourquoi*," he asked in French. Why?

She brought her gaze up to his. "Joseph Williams is from New Jersey."

She saw him add it up.

He looked behind her. "Where is Trevor?"

"They never came back from breakfast."

"Oh, fuck," he said. Then he fired off a quick order in French. The engines changed sound.

Hannah turned to leave.

"You cannot go alone."

"It's not your problem and I don't think I trust you."

"Well, fuck you then," he said in a soft voice. "But this is my ship and if my men are behaving rudely, I will want to talk to them."

"Curt," André snapped in French. Curt responded and moved to some controls.

André took her by the elbow, walking beside her. "The ship can make another eight hundred miles on the fuel we have. We will find a port where they will not be waiting."

Joseph Williams smiled as she walked first into the engine room, his two side kicks in the back.

"You're looking good, Mrs. Galban," he said. "I like the coloring. I was hoping we could talk."

"Why?" she asked. She held Trevor's 9mm at her side, finger on the trigger.

Williams was so unimpressed, he didn't even look at it.

The captain came in behind her and Williams stood straight.

"Captain," she said.

"*Qui?*"

"Are these the only three people who can run this engine room?"

"No. There is a backup if there are problems."

"If I said there were seven figures involved in watching my back, what would you say?"

"Fuck you. Keep your money. I have your back anyway."

"Good," she said. She hated guns. Always had. The boys respected that and kept them out of the house. She raised her weapon quick and shot Williams in the right kneecap without asking a question.

He screamed and dropped to the floor clutching his leg, blood between his fingers. His friends yelled and started to move toward her, all shouting en mass, the sound deafening over the engines.

She raised the gun toward them until they backed away.

"I have them covered," André said beside her. "Ask your questions."

She stepped forward to within easy reach of Williams, but he bled too badly to grab for her.

"I want you to consider something very carefully while you bleed," she said.

"You fucking bitch," he seethed through clenched teeth.

"You have another kneecap, two elbows, two feet and a head. I have fourteen rounds."

He glared at her.

"You know who they are, don't you?"

He was panting, drooling. "No."

She put the gun against his thigh. "Try again because the great state of New Jersey made their trial a media circus. You're from New Jersey? You heard or you lived in a hole."

He waited, out of breath, finally spitting an answer at her. "My cousin ran with Payday." He panted, his face pale. "It was a good job until yours finished it."

"What was your cousin's name?"

He paused. "Mike Morales."

She laughed at the irony. To come so far for the same names.

"One of the six. He was the look-out in the backyard. Your cousin shot Jayce in the face as he cleared the door. Four times. Jayce could have lived. He made to safety and your cousin took it away so he got a bullet in the head. You think what you are doing is some sort of revenge?"

"I want them to feel it," Williams sneered, spittle on his chin.

"And you know what? I don't lose the fights I pick." She cocked the gun. "If I miss the femoral, you die slower than Jayce or Mike. And these are warm waters, aren't they, Captain?"

"*Qui, assez chaud.*"

"I sent Payday to warm waters. What do you think are the chances for the son-of-a-bitch to actually be eaten by a shark? Did you know Payday was eaten by a shark? Not many people do."

"Yeah, I believe that, bitch. Your husband is fucking going to die for what he did. They both are."

"Going to," she said on a sigh. "Not dead yet."

He glared at her with hatred.

She squeezed real slow until the gun popped and he jerked. He screamed louder and bled more.

"Thirteen more," she said. "I can't kill your cousin but I can kill you by proxy and I swear to God if you hurt my men..."

"Stop," the man at the back right said. Hispanic with a perfect American accent.

"Shut up," Williams said.

"And the authorities, they're waiting for us?" she asked.

"No, just for them. He thought you would talk and give us away."

She stood up. "You were going to kill me, and turn them in?"

"It was $500,000."

He said it as if the motive should be obvious.

She took a step forward, around William's bloody mess on the floor. She reached up to yank the gold cross off his neck. It was almost two inches, depicting the crucifixion.

She looked at him, holding it up. "Catholic right?"

"So?"

"Your church has this thing about murdering unborn babies."

He stared at her, breathing heavy.

"I'm ten weeks pregnant. Kill the mother, kill the baby and you go straight to hell. Why don't you take a second to think about that one and then take me to my men?"

He paled. "You're pregnant? You're not lying?"

She raised the gun. "You can walk fine with a bullet in your shoulder."

"Go," André snapped.

She turned to look at him. "You knew. About me?"

"I suspected. A man is with a woman for three years and then needs to be married in a day, generally a reason. Let's go get them."

"Behind there," Jones said.

Two of André's loyal men came forward, pulling the crates away until a hatch not even four feet across became visible.

One of the men produced a screw driver and started opening it. He got the last screw out and the cover fell to the ground with a bang.

Trevor and Gavin were stacked in tight, their backs to each other, their hands behind their backs. Both their faces snapped up and they squinted to the light. Thick layers of duct tape covered their mouths.

The two men leaned in to grab Trevor by the shoulders, pulling him out and dropping him onto the deck clear of the cubby. While Gavin came out, André leaned over and yanked the tape off Trevor's face.

He took in a huge gulp of air, coughed a little and stared at the floor.

"Hannah?" he gasped.

"Right here," André said. "Shooting people who piss her off."

Trevor lowered his head to the deck. "Oh thank God. They said they threw her overboard."

She came forward to take André's place, kneeling down beside Trevor.

"I'm right here," she said, a hand to his bruised face.

André cut away the tape on his wrists and his arms popped apart, a hand jumped up to hold hers.

The backs of his, covered with nail marks matching Gavin's. They had tried to get each other out, clawing at each other until they bled.

He rolled onto his back, taking her hand with him, resting it on his chest, his eyes closed, his breathing hard.

He was bruised in the face, around the eyes. Blood matted part of his hair, his shirt, his nose. On the chest, seen in the V of his shirt, were more dark marks. Gavin looked the same.

She looked up to André. "The missionaries? They have a medic?"

"I believe so." He turned to Curt and spoke in French. Curt ran out of the room.

"I thought you were dead in the ocean," Trevor whispered.

"I thought you at least had Gavin with you."

"They jumped us. He knew us."

Gavin pointed to the ceiling. "That was me," he said. "Mike Morales. My shot. That was me."

"You look like shit," she said.

Trevor shifted his head and smiled at her. "You swore."

She pulled the ring off Trevor's finger, his head turned to face her, his breathing heavy. "Divorcing me?"

"The man who made these is the same man who orchestrated this."

He thought hard, breaths still deep, then pulled off hers with one hand, slapping it onto the deck. "That's fucking twisted," he chuckled.

A THIRD NEW BEGINNING

Trevor, thirty-three today, had been right on several points. She did have big brown eyes. She did have thick dark hair, already deep below her shoulders at two and a half and she had twisted him right around her little finger.

He picked her up off the bed where he had changed her, held her close and let her rest her head on his shoulder.

She called him 'dada' and he loved it.

"Pooh, dada."

"Ah, sorry." He smiled and went back to the bed for her Pooh bear.

He sat her on the side of the sink while he washed his hands, then picked her cooing little self back up, held her tight and moved through the house to the back porch.

The place was modest in its extravagance. Two stories with the rooms they needed and not one extra. The auto restoration shop half a mile away, *Juez y Proscritos*—their Judge & Outlaw, relocated. The Spanish they learned while with their babysitter for eight years had finally come in handy.

Five and half months pregnant, glowing and gorgeous, Hannah lifted Lacey's twin sister, Lucy into the sandbox and handed Lucy a shovel to toss dirt around.

Also big brown eyes. Also brown hair. Also had him tied right around her finger.

Both the mother and his daughters.

"Gavin called," she said, as she moved back through the door to get a pitcher of lemonade. "They're about ten minutes out."

Trevor put Lacey beside Lucy then checked the child gates. The porch wasn't high but they worried.

"Not even on time for my birthday, the bastard."

"He said Tia was settling Sarah down."

The first Sarah had been Gavin's four year old sister.

Trevor smiled as he made sure the BBQ was hot.

Gavin caught and tied just as tight. Where was his ten bucks now that Gavin found the only natural born girl in Costa Rica with blonde hair and light brown eyes?

"Can I ask you a question that has haunted me these years?"

Trevor looked up at his friend André. Curt was on the ground on his hands and knees, chasing Lacey while barking. Lacey loved it.

"Did you know she killed Payday Morgan?"

Surprised, Trevor stared. "How did you know about that?"

"The day we came for you. She used it as leverage to make sure they would cooperate. Then she shot them anyway."

Trevor thought about that, taking a drink of his beer. "I didn't know that."

"Sharing information was not priority that day."

Trevor thought. "Um…no. We didn't know. Not at first."

"She didn't tell you?"

"She was afraid to, but it didn't matter because she didn't. Not really. I think she still blames herself sometimes, but she didn't have a gun in hand." Trevor looked at André.

"Why does she think she did?"

"Information, which is what she was always good at getting. She sent some info to the right person and the right person did the rest."

"You loved her still, knowing she did this. "

He was smiling. "That was pretty much a done deal when she told a prison guard she was a fucking bitch to be reckoned with."

"What you have been doing with her," André said with a smirk. "It seems to agree with her. She is more beautiful than ever."

Trevor pursed his lips over a smile and looked at his friend. He pointed at her over by Tia. Hannah was bouncing eight-month old Sarah.

"You see that, Captain? That is my wife and my son." He looked at André. "We just found out. His name is Jayce."

"After your brother," André said.

"That same night in the cemetery when we decided to do what we did, we also decided to have seven kids between us, four girls and three boys. Both of us understanding that, of course, you can't really predict that. We agreed to keep trying until everyone was honored. My wife there, thought we needed to get started."

"Hey," she called across the deck. "What are you talking about?"

Trevor smiled. "We were discussing how fat you are getting."

She glared at him, smiled wicked and held up a small box in the palm of her hand. "Birthday boy, talk like that and you might not get your present."

"That's my present?" he asked pointing at the three inch, red bow on top. "I happen to know your net worth and I think you could do better than that."

Smiling, everyone laughing and watching, she took the lid off.

"Hey, mine," he laughed.

She reached in, pulling out a single key and held it up.

They took the kids, Lacey to André, Lucy to Curt and lined up in front of the heavy dark wood garage door. Gavin held Sarah with Tia beside him.

"Are you going to give me a clue, wife?"

"Open it," she smiled.

"Um huh," Trevor mumbled as he moved to the lock. He twisted the key, it popped and he dropped them to the ground. Moving to the center handle, he paused for effect, then tossed the garage door up, freezing the second the contents came into site.

"Shit," Gavin whispered, handing Sarah to Tia and moving forward. "Is that it?"

Trevor looked at her, paused, then looked at the red car in front of him, as pristine as the day it came off the line. Shiny paint with hood scoops staring back at him. The symbol GTO sat in the characteristic bumper.

The license plate read MYOTLWS.

Trevor stepped forward to place his hand on the hood, feeling the reality of the cool metal. "Is this it?"

"Yes," she said, a hand on her tummy, her head tilted. "It was impounded years ago and eventually sold at auction to a collector. It wasn't hard to find the buyer and outbid his imagination."

He turned to look at her, feeling awe on his breath. Gavin came in to move toward the back, looking in the windows. He pulled open the driver's side door to the familiar creak that had only ever belonged to this car.

"This was the best car we ever did," Trevor said, looking at it.

"You taught me how to drive stick in it," she smiled.

"Yeah," he laughed. "That was a lot of fun."

"It's *our* car," she said. "It belongs to our history, the three of us."

He walked over to her. In front of the laughing people he called family, he kissed her hard.

"No, it's a part of our past. We're just getting started."

ABOUT THE AUTHOR

Award-winning author, Jacqui Jacoby lives and writes in the beauty of Northern Arizona. Currently adjusting to being an empty nester with her first grandchild to draw her pictures, Jacqui is a self-defense hobbyist. Having studied martial arts for numerous years she retired in 2006 from the sport, yet still brings strength she learned from the discipline to her heroines. She is a working writer, whose career includes writing books, teaching online and live workshops and penning short nonfiction.

Follow her at www. jacquijaxjacoby.com

www.jaxsmovielist.blogspot.com

Twitter: JaxJacoby

Facebook: Jacqui Jax Jacoby

Google + Jacqui Jacoby

Instagram: JacquiJaxJacoby

Pinterest: Jacqui Jacoby

ALSO BY JACQUI JACOBY

NOW AVAILABLE

Dead Men Seal the Deal

Bystander

Magic Man

Dead Men Play the Game

With a Vengeance

Books in The Dead Men Series:

Dead Men Play the Game

Dead Men Seal the Deal

Dead Men Feel the Heat

Dead Men Heal Slowly

A Collection of Dead Men: 13 short stories

AADEN'S HOPE

© 2006 Jacqui Jacoby, Body Count Productions, Inc.
Available September, 2016
Enjoy the following excerpt from Aaden's Hope

Two o'clock was not too late to get up when you had gone to bed at six. No good days work could be claimed here. Only a party with Piper that had been too much fun followed by more fun at home.

Well her home, he thought, face down on the bed, his arms under the pillow.

He was three weeks running in occupying this spot.

Sighing, he knew he had to get up. He blinked a couple times to test for a hangover, being assured he was spared.

Aaden Muñoz started to stir. The apartment wasn't big and the aroma of coffee was enough to make him move.

Only he didn't have any jobs today.

He didn't have any for the rest of the week.

Rolling over to stare at the ceiling, he thought about the fact, neither of those things would change unless he did something about it.

Hired man. Helper. Man of all trades. It wasn't a prestigious title, but it paid the bills and was flexible enough to keep him happy.

Smiling, he finally got up naked, he used the bathroom then made his way to the kitchen. Piper wasn't paying attention to him so he poured his own coffee black, got a bowl of cereal and snaked a banana.

Piper wasn't a girlfriend. She knew that as well as he did. She was a good time, though and he had enjoyed sleeping in her bed more than the single he had in his one-room studio across town.

She was sitting on the edge of the couch, watching the TV. The short multi-colored kimono she wore around the apartment, hung around her shoulders.

"What are you doing?" he asked.

She turned to blink her green eyes at him. Her face was pale, her expression shocked.

He sat down beside her, his bowl held in front of him, one foot on the crate she used as a coffee table.

"Have you seen this?" she asked.

"Have I seen what?"

"It's all over the place," she said with a shaky voice, pointing at the TV. "Australia, Russia. It's even started here."

"What are you talking about?" He asked, looking at her.

"People are dying. A lot of people are dying."

"People die all the time and it's usually on the news."

"In Australia they said over half the people are gone. It started there."

He lowered his bowl. "What are you talking about?"

"I'm serious. They said it's in Florida now and moving. We're not supposed to panic. Just stay calm and do what we always do."

He looked at her with narrowed eyes, then turned toward the screen, listening to the blonde beauty offer the information with a half-smile.

The Ross Valley Epidemic originated in the Australian Outback, a result of human interaction with the wildlife using chemicals and pesticides still under investigation.

It will kill—in minutes, hours or days, depending on the host.

It is estimated that before a cure is developed, it will wipe over 60% of the world's population.

"This is bullshit," he said. "Their ratings just went up."

"What if it's true? Can it get here?"

"No, it can't get here. You're scared for nothing."

He finished eating, stood, took his bowl to the sink and cleaned it. He walked back to the bedroom, thinking the whole time. He got dressed in the clothes he wore yesterday.

"We should go camping," he said as he came into the kitchen area. "Do you want to go camping?"

"You want to what? There is a problem in the world and you want to pitch a tent?"

"I know this place. It's kinda nice. It's got cabins so there isn't any pitching. Bathrooms are good and at sometimes, the people that run it, they use the lodge for meals and stuff. I've been there a few times."

"What is that going to solve?" She snapped.

"It will get us out of the city while the world decides what it wants."

"I don't camp," she said, turning to light one of the cigarettes he hated.

"I do. I can help you figure it out. I do this all the time."

They really didn't know enough about each other besides positions. And she was pretty damn good at those.

"Come on, Piper. We'll have fun."

"You go have fun. I have to call my mom."

And that was enough of a break-up for him. This was never till death do they part or anything that resembled it.

He cleared out what little there was in here of him, put the stuff in a plastic grocery bag and was already calculating his finances as he headed for the door.

He heard her talking soft as he opened the door. She didn't stop to look up. He didn't offer any good wishes.

As she walked up, he realized she was the first person he had seen since the camp ground owners had left on day two.

"Hi," she smiled, holding the young kid close on her hip. He looked like her with the blue eyes and the long, thin brown hair.

He pulled on his line before he had a catch, sticking the edge of the pole into the soft sand.

"Have you been here long?" she asked.

"I don't know. I don't have a calendar and my phone died awhile back. I'm Aaden."

She looked around. "It doesn't seem like there's enough to live on."

"We got this," he pointed to the lake. And there is a store about three miles. Owners disappeared awhile back from the sign on the door. They left the back door open. I've been getting what I need and fixing what's broken to pay for it. Who is this?" Aaden asked, nodding at the kid.

She smiled down at the child. "Jared, say hi to Aaden"

The kid burrowed into her shoulder, making Aaden smile.

"I'm Lexi," she said. "I was in San Francisco and this happened. I drove for a while then came here. The world's gone crazy. I saw people fall."

Aaden didn't respond to that. "No one's falling here. I can get you set in a cabin."

He got her to a cabin, got the supplies out of the lodge and made the beds for her and Jared.

She kept her distance for a few days and he didn't mind. He made extra food, they chatted. Jared ran around the green.

A few days later, when Lexi and Jared started stripping down to their unmentionables three days in a row, while Aaden sat on the bank, he thought things might take a turn in an unexpected direction. Her wet thin T-shirt didn't require a lot of imagination.

She came out of the water, holding Jared's hand, smiling shyly.

"It's Jared's nap time. He usually falls asleep right away and is a deep sleeper."

"Really?" Aaden asked. He wasn't quite sure what he thought of the situation. He wasn't opposed to casual sex but it was something he had to be in the mood for. Caulking up bedpost notches wasn't his style.

Besides, she might be looking for a hero in a world she saw go wild.

He went to his cabin, she went to hers.

Twenty minutes later, she came over to his, leaving the door open wide. He sat on the edge of the bed, his guitar on his knee.

She sat beside him while he recognized he was running out of time to decide before it was decided for him. She reached up to push his hair back from his forehead with her fingers, her hand curving behind his neck.

His gaze snapped up, his hand following. "You're burning."

"No, I'm not. I just got out of the lake, that's all."

"And that would cool you off." Staring her in the face he saw a distance in her eyes that didn't seemed to match, a pinkness to her soft skin. He stood up to lean the guitar in the corner.

"Where you going?" she smiled.

But the smile wasn't the same as it had been. Her stare was glazed.

"I have an idea," he said. "Why don't we go next door, you won't have to worry about Jared and we can take a nap."

"Take a nap?" she asked.

"Yeah," he said with a big grin he wasn't feeling. "I'm real tired, I'd love a nap. With you right there."

She stood, swaying a little and he led her back to her cabin.

Except that Lexi was dead by morning.

Made in the USA
San Bernardino, CA
11 June 2016